AND FILIGREE

FLASH AND FILIGREE

Grove Press
New York

First published in 1958 by Coward-McCann, Inc.
First Grove Press paperback edition published in 1996

Published simultaneously in Canada
Printed in the United States of America

Library of Congress Cataloging-in-Publication Data

Southern, Terry.
Flash and filigree: a novel / by Terry Southern. —1st Grove Press pbk. ed.
p. cm.
ISBN 0-8021-3430-0
I. Title.
PS3569. O8F53 1996
813'.54—dc20 95-49491

Grove Press
841 Broadway
New York, NY 10003

10 9 8 7 6 5 4 3 2 1

FOR CAROL

breadth and purity of line. The white pebble drive curves graciously upward, broad in pleasing compliment to the deep and near-blue verdure of the grounds. There is expanse and coolness here truly of the country. A travesty on nature. An artifice so masterfully contrived that, like the parks of Madrid or a Japanese garden, it holds a novel and fascinating beauty.

The width of these grounds is secured by trim footwalks of glazed cement and rounded gravel-paths that trail back through fragile-leafed jacaranda trees grown heavy with lavender blossoms above the white low-set benches of a natural stone. And across these benches the shadows lie cool and dark in the soft spring morning, stretching down from overhead where only the wind is heard, rustling the high boughs of cypress and pine.

In quiet relief to the broad approach is the Clinic. The flat, heavy cream-stucco of the Clinic is the essence of modern architectural propriety and its modest substantial proportions already suggest the knowledge, the strict and unassuming skill for which it is renowned.

At exactly 10.30, after a few minutes in the outer reception room, a young man was shown into the office of Dr Frederick Eichner, world's foremost dermatologist.

These rooms strike a free and immediate rapport with the whole of the Clinic and its surrounding grounds. Light, flat surfaces, an economy of angles. Windows here are low and expansive, their drapes restless in the soft play of Pacific breeze that stirs through the quiet room with the fragrance of a tropical garden.

Dr Eichner, a grey distinguished man, was at his desk. He looked up into the visitor's face as he entered, then referred once briefly to the suede agenda before him. 'Mr Treevly, I believe.' And saying this, he stood extending his hand and, with a subsequent gesture, indicated a chair drawn near the desk.

'Yes, Doctor,' said the other, taking the Doctor's hand before seating himself, 'and allow me to say that I feel . . . *privileged* to consult you. I know, of course, that you are the outstanding dermatologist of our time.'

Dr Eichner looked at him narrowly, giving the tribute an only slightly personable smile.

'That's very kind of you,' he said. And, clearing his throat, he sat down.

The patient was a thin man of about thirty. An aquiline nose and deep-set eyes, his dark hair was fine, receding slightly at the temples. He was perhaps a handsome man, in an anaemic and quasi-aristocratic way. Felix Treevly.

Dr Eichner sat quietly, his white drawn hands clasped, resting on the desk, his lips parted in an almost weary smile, perhaps only tolerant of his own opening cliché, inevitable, as he asked:

'And what, Mr Treevly, seems to be the trouble?'

'Yes,' replied the young man, sitting forward in the chair at first, then back easily, crossing his legs. 'Well, I don't think it's much really. I have, or rather *did* have . . . a certain lesion. A lesion which wouldn't, or at least *didn't*

'May I,' interrupted the Doctor again, now with the faintest pained smile, '. . . may I see it?'

'Of course,' said the other, speaking pleasantly; but he followed the remark with a look of extreme care. 'I should like to give you some *particulars* . . . which may facilitate, or rather, have *some-bearing-on* . . . the diagnosis.'

'Yes,' said Dr Eichner after a pause. 'Yes, of course,' and he leaned back, a little heavily, perhaps even in resignation.

'As I say,' the young man went on, '. . . it began about a year ago, simply an irritation at first—on the fleshy hinder part, or calf, of the left leg. A small boil, actually, a cystic mass—or *wen* if you like, extremely small, no larger than the common variety of facial pustule. I noticed it bathing; it hadn't *bothered* me otherwise. And when I got out of the bath, I opened it with a needle—sterilized of course—pressed out the secretion, and swabbed it down with tincture of merthiolate: two per cent solution.' He shrugged, smiling slightly and continued. 'I didn't notice it again until my bath the next evening, naturally I removed it, and followed with a second application of merthiolate.'

The young man's eyes met the Doctor's as he spoke, and they were sharply blue and perceptive, though from moment to moment across his expression passed the light veil of selflessness and absence that can come to one who recalls and presents details exactly.

Opposite now, the Doctor sat as weighted, without motion except for the fingers that played in slowly varying design over the golden tip of an automatic pencil he held in his hand. And wide behind the two, the windows opened on to a fine spring day, a rich sun, and the soft sound of the morning wind.

'On the following night,' Mr Treevly continued, 'I found it the same as I had on the previous evening, that is to say : *open*, with secretion. And the same again on the next night, and so on for a week. Each night, of course, I repeated the treatment. By the end of the week there had been almost no change. The opening of the pustule was, if anything, larger, and the secretion . . . proportionately less. The next day — that is to say, eight days after its appearance — I began treating with mercuric oxide under a sterile compress, which I redressed *each night*, after my bath. I continued this treatment for two weeks, during which time there *was* an appreciable change : the opening had become noticeably larger, though as before, the secretion proportionately less. *Now* the opening was about the size of a match-head. The swelling around it was larger than before, of course, but by no means as largely increased in proportion as had the opening. *Obviously,* local treatment wasn't getting-the-job-done. So, I gave up the dressing and compress, did what I could during the next few weeks to step up my metabolism : plenty of bed-rest, hot baths, regular meals, and the rest of it.'

smile, which Mr Treevly could not have missed.

'Probably it annoys you,' said the young man after a moment, 'my use, or misuse as it were, of your own idiom; but the fact is I'm doing my best to make you understand certain particulars which are sure to have some bearing on the case.'

'Of course,' said the Doctor, flushing a little, coughing. 'No, on the contrary. It's always beneficial when a patient can describe symptoms objectively, *and*—' he cleared his throat on the word, at the same time gestured to show that it was nothing, '*and* . . . with accuracy. Certainly. Now, after you stopped the oxide treatment?'

'Yes,' Mr Treevly continued, stiffly at first, then relaxing again. 'Well, as I say, I *stopped* using the dressing and compress. At the same time, I began to make a point of wearing only white cotton next to the lesion—white cotton socks, extra long, of course—had body rubdowns twice a week, eliminated nicotine, alcohol, caffeine, tannic acid and so on from the diet, and did what else I could to fight the virus systemically.' Here he shrugged, smiling, almost distantly, somewhat in preoccupation now. 'But it was persistent, you see. And actually, it was taking up a lot of my attention, a lot of my thoughts. Not that it was painful. No, no, I can't say that it was really painful.' He shook his head as if to impress this, 'Oh, sometimes there was slight irritation, an itching, and a general soreness to the touch, granted. But it wasn't really disturbing in the physical sense. It was the persistence of it, you see . . .'

Mr Treevly paused and proffered the Doctor a cigarette, which the latter declined, then he continued, speaking for the moment with a cigarette between his lips, laughing a little. 'You can understand *that*, how it could be disturbing : psychologically, I mean; the persistence . . .'

'Oh yes,' said Dr Eichner. 'Yes, of course.'

'Well,' the other went on, 'after four weeks of fighting the virus systemically, there was nothing to show for it.' He broke off again and smiled, a bit sheepishly, or even, it may have seemed, with a certain conscious modesty. 'Yes, it was still there, all right. Wider now, about the size of a pencil-top, a quarter-inch or so deep, soft, but not discharging. I decided I was worrying too much about it, decided to put it out of my mind. After all, it could be, to a degree at least, *psychosomatic*. It was making a fool of me, or rather *I* was making a fool of myself about *it*. So I cauterized it—with a small silver plate, electrically heated—and then I ignored it, forgot about it completely. Didn't bother to look at it when I bathed, and I stopped wearing the white cotton socks—not deliberately, of course, but I was simply indifferent to colour, just took whatever came to hand. I didn't have occasion to see it again for six months. When I did, the opening then was about the size of a small coin, and almost an inch deep. I packed it with a cancer culture—cerebral cancer—and covered it over with a Band-Aid.'

going out together. Naturally he often shows me the work he's doing. This time it happened to be with cerebral cancer . . . and there were these tubes, or *vials* if you like, of culture sitting in the rack. Oh, I'd noticed them before, of course, without thinking anything in particular about it. This night though—he'd been working with some pretty nasty stains—and he was a long time in washing up. So, while I was alone, waiting for him there in the lab, I happened to think of the lesion. It may have been smarting slightly, I don't remember, but anyway I had a look. "Still *there*, are you?" I said. "Just sitting there all alone with nothing to do? Well, now, we'll have to do something about that, won't we?" And I took down one of the tubes of culture, scooped some out with my finger and filled up the lesion with it, packed it right in — about the colour and consistency of wet yeast it was; do you know it at all, by the way? Oh, I suppose you do, of course. Anyway, I sealed it over with a *Band-Aid*.'

'With a what?' asked the Doctor, frowning.

'A Band-Aid,' replied the young man easily. 'You know, a small adhesive compress. I'd been carrying a pack since the earlier treatments.'

'Yes, I see,' said the Doctor.

'And so . . .' Mr Treevly shrugged. '*I* went on about

my own affairs. Didn't pay the slightest attention to it, not the *slightest*. In fact, I didn't see it again for another long period—about four months, actually. It was covered with the compress, which I managed to keep out of the water so it wouldn't come off when I was taking a bath. Then I had a look, quite by accident as a matter of fact, when the compress finally *did* slip off as I was dressing. Two weeks ago. That's when I made the appointment. I told the girl—your secretary, I suppose—that it wasn't urgent, and she suggested this date. At the time, I didn't realize it was so far ahead, but she said you were very busy. So *I* took the first date she suggested, without really realizing, you see, how far *ahead* it was. I had a look at the lesion this morning. It seems completely healed over.'

Then Mr Treevly leaned forward. 'I'll just show you,' he said, and raised his eyes to poise a look, almost of challenge, at the Doctor.

Dr Eichner didn't move for a moment, his head resting on his hand. 'Yes,' he said finally, getting to his feet. 'Yes. If you'll . . . just step over here to the light—perhaps you'd better lie on that couch . . .'

Mr Treevly quickly removed his shoes and trousers and lay down on the low brown leather sofa where he seemed to hold himself rather stiffly, staring at the ceiling like a man in a trance. Dr Eichner examined the lesion. On the inner side of the left calf, quite near the knee, was a little region of very slight redness, the skin almost imperceptibly drawn towards the trace of a small flat scar. The Doctor touched it with one finger, then with several outstretched, gently pressing the surrounding area. It seemed to have

Mr Treevly was sitting on the edge of the sofa, bending over, putting on his shoes, when the Doctor crossed the room again, pausing just momentarily at his desk where he picked up a cupped onyx paperweight holding a few clips and rubber bands. He emptied these onto the desk and walked toward the sofa, taking out his handkerchief as he did and wrapping it around the coloured stone.

'Well, I thought as much,' said the young man with what sounded like a chuckle, distant, head bent, fingers working at the lace, '. . . but *I* always say it's better to play safe in matters like this.'

'Yes, of course,' said the Doctor and, as he spoke, standing very close, he brought the padded weight down sharply across the back of the young man's skull.

Mr Treevly crumpled, but before he could slip to the floor, Dr Eichner pushed him back onto the sofa. Then he walked rapidly to his desk, undoing the handkerchief from the paperweight and replacing it, with the clips and rubber bands, on the desk. He sat down, took a sheet of memo-paper and his pen.

You are lying, he wrote. *You are a psychopathic liar. If you ever come back here, I will turn you over to the police. I warn you: stay away, and leave me alone; or you will find yourself in very serious trouble —*

At that instant the inter-office phone rang. Dr Eichner started, crumpled the paper and threw it in the waste basket. He picked up the phone immediately. 'Yes?' He was almost shouting. 'What? *No.* No, Miss Smart; now listen to me: there's a stretcher-case in my office. I want him taken to one of the day-rooms in the West Wing. He'll come around soon; he's intoxicated. Do you understand? And have my car sent. Yes, right away; I'm going home. Yes, of course, cancel them! Have the car sent round now. *Yes, yes, at once!*'

CHAPTER II

'DAFFYS will do for Harrison if it's really going to *spoil* anything.' Barbara Mintner spoke brightly from the day-room window, leaning out with a smile for one last press of the sill against her trim abdomen.

Just below, puttering in the strip of turned soil, Garcia raised his dark face to hers and again she was standing straight and proper, her slight figure starched a delicate confectionery in fresh nurse's habit, framed a merciless white, indomitable, against the mauve grey of the day-room walls.

'We see,' said the Mexican gardener, trying to smile a little.

'Garcia, *please*,' said Miss Mintner in her child's voice, pouting her lips at him, then coming forward on the sill again all confidence and animation. 'She's going Sunday. It's true this time!'

Garcia tu [illegible]

[illegible] time, Garcia,' Miss Mintner pouting, almost pleading, 'it really is! And wouldn't it be a shame not to have them on the last two days, after doing it all along!'

'Three day,' said Garcia, 'three day, count today.'

'All right, silly, three days. Please try! It doesn't have to be freesias for Harrison, but *please* get the roses. Remember, just two more days!'

'Two day,' said the gardener shaking his head, looking back down to where his hand turned the dark loam with a trowel.

Before Barbara Mintner could follow it up, the West Hall door sounded opening, and swift creped-steps could be heard in the corridor outside the day-room wall.

'Please, Garcia,' she said quickly, making her voice a stage whisper, 'you *won't* be sorry, I promise you.' And she brought the two panelled-windows in slowly, smiling a secret at him as he watched from below, herself now on tip-toe, leaning forward slightly, the motion timed so that she was just closing the latch when Head Nurse Eleanor Thorne swung the day-room door open.

'And what's Mister Garcia up to now?' said Nurse Thorne taking it all in without breaking her stride before she reached the centre of the room.

'Oh, he's such a baby,' said Barbara Mintner turning to half face her. 'Afraid someone's going to spoil his precious playthings.'

Eleanor Thorne scoffed. 'I dare say. I'm only too glad you didn't say *work*things!'

The soft brilliance of the Pacific morning lay behind Barbara Mintner and etched a golden haze along the proud lines of her head and shoulders.

'Your hair is quite nice that way,' said Eleanor Thorne abruptly and, quickly rushing on with a gesture toward the low leather couch where Mr Treevly lay: 'How is he?'

'He's coming around,' said Miss Mintner, 'while ago his respiration—' and even as she pronounced the word, Mr Treevly raised his head, then lowered it again very slowly.

'Feeling better?' said Nurse Thorne, walking briskly toward his couch against the far wall.

'It's my head,' said Mr Treevly, passing a hand over his closed eyes.

Near the window, Barbara Mintner muffled a snicker.

'I shouldn't wonder,' said Nurse Thorne archly, after throwing a sharp glance at Miss Mintner.

'I'm going to lunch now,' she continued to the girl, turning and stepping precisely past her. 'I'll stop at the Dispensary and have Albert bring over some bromide. I'm going to the cafeteria, and then to Bullock's . . .' She finished in a masculine tone over her shoulder in the open door: 'If the bromide doesn't bring it off, give him a sodo-injection. Two c.c.'s. I'll be back at 12.20.'

'Yes, Miss Thorne,' said Babs Mintner, lowering her eyes as if she had been painfully kissed.

to look out of the window, across the rolling lawn and through the trees beyond. She hummed softly to herself.

Mr Treevly slowly pulled himself up, sat on the edge of the couch, his face in his hands. Suddenly he lurched forward, getting to his feet, then fell back bodily onto the couch, catching himself with one hand.

'Where is the Doctor?' he cried. 'Where is Dr Eichner? What *happened*?'

Miss Mintner gave a start, involuntarily shrank back toward the window; then, as quickly, she crossed the room to his couch.

'Now, please,' she was firm, 'please lie *quietly*. Everything is all right.' She put her hands on both his shoulders and pushed down on him. Mr Treevly resisted.

'What's the matter?' he repeated, looking around rather wildly. 'Where is the Doctor?'

'Nothing's the matter,' Miss Mintner shrilled. 'Now *please* lie back! I'm going to give you something and you'll be perfectly all right.' She looked anxiously toward the door, speaking half aloud. 'Oh, where is that *boy*?'

Mr Treevly shook her away violently. 'What's going on here?' he cried. 'What's up!' There seemed to be pain and a certain desperation in his voice.

Miss Mintner dropped her hands and stepped back

abruptly, so angry she could cry.

'Nothing happened I tell you! You had too-much-to-drink and now you're acting like a baby!' Then in a burst of indignation, she came forward, cross enough with herself to slap him, and began to push on his shoulders again. But her anger was spent in the gesture and there only remained a tearful petulence. 'Please lie back!' she said. '*Please.*' She drew the word out in a sob.

Mr Treevly made an odd grimace, felt his head with outstretched fingers, then closed his eyes and lay back, one hand to his brow.

Barbara Mintner sighed, not quite audibly, touched her hair and dabbed lightly at her moist temples. Suddenly she shot a fearful glance to the window where she had whispered with Garcia. She moved as if to determine whether or not he was there now, listening.

'Is this the Hauptman Clinic?' asked Mr Treevly without raising his head.

Miss Mintner stopped, stood looking at him from mid-floor. 'Yes,' she answered, as caution and uneasiness crept back into her face.

'I'm a patient of Dr Eichner,' said the young man evenly.

'Yes, that's right,' said Miss Mintner. She glanced at the door. 'Where *is* that little fool!' she said under her breath.

Mr Treevly raised his head, his eyes open wide. 'You know then?' He had risen to one elbow.

'Yes, of course,' said Miss Mintner moving toward him, and again as if to prevent his getting off the couch, she put one hand on his shoulder. 'Now please...' she said in the tone she had used with the gardener. 'Please lie back!'

and stopped short.

'Really,' she said, turning suddenly in tears at the unfairness of it, 'I've never seen anything like it. You're a bundle of never-ends! A person would think you'd been taking benzidrene, instead of . . . instead of . . . *whisky* . . . and goodness knows what else!' she added with forced contempt, her hand just touching the knob of the door as Mr Treevly slumped back to a lying position on the couch, his hands covering his face.

Standing at the door in silence, putting a handkerchief to her soft wet eyes, she watched him narrowly. 'I don't care,' she said half-aloud in bitterness, 'it just isn't fair!'

On the couch, Mr Treevly groaned painfully.

And watching his helplessness now, Miss Mintner began to feel herself once more at the helm of the situation. She eased toward him from the door, still clutching the small handkerchief in her hand. When she was quite near the couch, Mr Treevly spoke in a broken whisper. 'Something is wrong, do you understand? I have a pain in my head. Would you please tell me where Dr Frederick Eichner is?'

Miss Mintner drew herself up. 'Dr Eichner has gone home,' she said imperiously. 'He left full instructions about you, and if you will just lie quietly until the wardboy comes from the dispensary with something to make you feel a lot better . . .'

'Gone *home*!' cried Treevly bolting upright. 'What do you mean gone home? What *time* is it?' He got to his feet unsteadily, warding her off with his hand. 'What time is it?' he demanded.

'Listen,' said Miss Mintner in an outraged girlish threat, '*I told you . . .*'

'What time is it!' Mr Treevly shouted.

Miss Mintner's face grew scarlet; she looked as if she were going to burst. Then she turned on her heel and walked straight to the door. 'All right! All right, if you won't co-operate . . . then do what you want to!' She flung open the door and turned to face him, her great eyes terrible now, blinded with tears and rage. '*Goddamn you*!' she said and slammed the door behind her.

In the hall however, standing with the door behind her, she dropped her face in her hands. Her slight shoulders bunched and shaking with dry sobs, she leaned back against the door. Then, an extraordinary thing happened. The door, although she had violently slammed it shut behind her, had failed to catch, and had, in fact, by the force of the slamming, rebounded to a quarter-open position; so that the girl now, having already through sightless anguish improperly reckoned the distance between herself and the door, came tumbling backward into the day-room.

Mr Treevly, standing by the couch in a wild daze, his fingers frozen half run through his thin hair, looked on at once in disbelief and then in something rising to savage reproach.

'What's going on!' he demanded. 'What's up!'

opened onto a blazing patio and a maze of breezeways, all leading to other departments of the Clinic in the opposite wing, and holding, each at its end with the same screened door to the sun, a plaque of high burnished light.

Miss Mintner crossed unerringly, rushing sightless through the right turns, only slowing herself when she was at last past the far screen and inside the other building. Here, she dropped her hands to her side and walked rapidly, eyes high and straight ahead, till she reached the ladies' room where she turned in quickly, crossed the tile floor past the lavatories, entered a booth and locked the door behind her. There she sat, crying audibly for five minutes before she heard someone else come into the lavatories; and then she began to pull herself together. Eleanor Thorne? Barbara sat very still. She could just make out the hands of her tiny watch. 12.10. Nurse Thorne would be back in ten minutes. Outside the booth a lavatory tap sounded in a rush of water. Under the covering noise Miss Mintner leaned forward, her eye near the crack of the door. But too late! Whoever it was had stepped away, drying hands, and was now actually leaving. She heard the outer door open and close . . . or had someone else come in? She listened intently, staring at the black gloss of the door in front of her. Gradually she had the sensation that she could wee-wee. She leaned back quietly, listening. No one. They were gone. How quickly too! It must have been a patient, she thought, the nurses dallied so.

It was 12.15 when Miss Mintner came out of the lavatory, and she looked as fresh and sweet as ever, except that her eyes were pinched and red. But she had retouched her whole appearance, had even, within the limits of its required shortness, changed the order of her hair.

All smiles now on her way to the dispensary, she passed several patients and two or three nurses from other wards; then, at one blind turning, she almost crashed into heavy Beth Jackson of gyno, senior service nurse at the Clinic.

They spoke together hurriedly, Miss Mintner in confidence, as a little girl breathless in the great woman's presence, giving an awed account of what had happened in the day-room, and Nurse Jackson, understanding now and in genuine sympathy at what was inferred: the very deliberate unfairness of it. Shaking her head slowly, her small eyes darkly grave, she almost drew the child to her bosom. But they neither mentioned Eleanor Thorne by name.

Mr Edwards, the pharmacist, was not at the Dispensary. His nephew, Ralph, was there, sitting behind the counter reading a book. Ralph Edwards was studying pharmacy in the University and often visited his uncle at the Clinic, but he had never, so far as Miss Mintner could know, been left there alone, in charge of the Dispensary.

She stood at the counter and pretended not to notice when the young man looked up, already smiling as if there shock as had he simply said outright: 'Yes, this is something we have to do, but if I had you in the back seat of my room-mate's convertible, you'd be panting hot by now!' It was intolerable.

'Mr Edwards,' she said coolly, stating her business.

'That's me,' said the young man, even half winking. He leaned toward her on the counter, arched his brow in mock disappointment. 'I thought you knew.'

'I don't know to what you're referring,' said Miss Mintner, not looking his way. She fought down an urge to touch her hair. 'Where is the pharmacist?' she said, and with a surprising effort, she rechannelled the other impulse into turning her head and giving the young man a very icy stare.

And so he began to cool, either in fear of causing his uncle some embarrassment, or in real offence. He straightened up. 'He was called out,' he said moving back to the chair, '. . . on an emergency. He and Albert went with Dr Evans. They should be back any time now.' He sat with the open book on his lap, pretending to regard Miss Mintner curiously, as she appeared not to be listening. 'If it's nothing that has to be compounded, of course,' he went on after a moment, 'I can get it for you myself.'

Not wearing a tie, she thought, a grown man; and needing a shave. She guessed this without looking, only feeling at once a thousand stiff prickles on her own soft face.

'Bromide powder,' she said. 'And a small bottle of distilled water.'

The young man stood up, setting a bottle of the water on the counter as he did. 'How much bromide?'

Miss Mintner hesitated. 'They're right there,' she said, pointing and, painfully then, as at a loss with his dullness, 'in that blue box on the second shelf. Just give me one of those packages.'

She averted her eyes from his smile as he crossed to the shelf and took a small glassine envelope from the box.

'Yes,' he said looking quizzical, 'that would be about a half gramme, wouldn't it?' He handed it over giving her his devastating grin as he did. 'Or seven-point-six grains.'

She took it from his hand at once, snatched up the bottle of water. 'Thank you,' she said airily, as though it were only her breeding that said it, and she turned away with a toss of her head. With her hair so short, the gesture was grotesque.

She marched back to the day-room, saying to herself most of the way: *What an absolute fool he is!* Halfway down the West Wing corridor she saw the day-room door, open as she had left it; and slowing her steps now, she began to collect herself. She would take no more abuse from this one, nor yet would she lose control of herself again.

She entered the day-room with the grace of a virgin queen, sweeping directly to a side table where she set down the bottle and powder, only realizing then she had not brought a glass. But this was as nothing to the sudden

She turned back to the couch where Mr Treevly had lain. Briefly, in starting to sit down, she put her hand on the raised headrest, then her whole body went suddenly stiff, throwing up one hand to block the scream in her throat and slowly turning the other, palm up as she closed her eyes quickly tight against the heavy, covering blood on her hand where it had touched the couch. She made a strangling sound and tore out of the room a few steps west into the hall away from the dancing light, to a booth with an open phone inside. She frantically dialled Dr Eichner's home number. Waiting, she held off the offending hand, outthrust now against the door of the booth.

'Hello, Doctor? DOCTOR?'

As Miss Mintner waited, not understanding, the screen at the far end of the hall, like a rose window of thin spun copper, was burst aside, banging against the wall of the corridor, and Albert, the ward-boy, raced toward her from the patio, his white face strained to wildness.

A ward-boy, he was actually a middle-aged man, terribly dwarfed and stone deaf, with a speech impediment that agonizingly muddled his every word. He stopped short before Miss Mintner breathing like a tempest, his whole aspect shot with fear and panic.

'Dey lubing for ub!' he cried and began to rattle the

handle of the door violently.

'Wait a sec, Bert,' said Miss Mintner, not bothering to take her mouth from the phone, '. . . something's up. Hello! Hello, Doctor?' But she opened the door to Albert and held out one arm for him as though he were coming to nest. Without a word, he seized her around the waist with his tiny, thick arms and began to pull at her viciously. 'Twenty-eight!' he shouted. 'TWENTY-EIGHT IN HEMORRHAGE!'

'Wait up, Bert,' said Miss Mintner, 'it's Fred—Dr Eichner,' and for a minute she managed to keep his hold tentative; but suddenly his arms were locked around her waist like a steel garter, mouth shouting against her chest, his chin digging into the ribs. Miss Mintner clutched at the sill and the open door as she was torn bodily from the booth. The phone jerked out of her hand with a crash and they went reeling onto the corridor floor. Albert was on his feet at once, trying to get her up with short ineffectual kicks and little tugs at her hair and dress. Miss Mintner fought back like a cornered cat, threshing her tiny feet about and striking at his face with the blood-covered hand, until she was up and running for the door, with Albert behind, driving her on, arms flailing above, while now his blood-stained face was dead and impassive, like a wooden mask.

shaded front veranda, waiting for his car to be sent round.

Looking over the sweep of lawn and the gravel drive, past the tight footwalks and overhanging trees, he could see beyond to Wilshire Boulevard where the stirring smoke and dust of property improvements wound up unending through the day.

At the corner of the building then, the car appeared, a white-frocked garage attendant at the wheel, slithering the heavy car on the rounded curve. The Doctor raised his eyes like an alerted animal: the soft contusion of gravel under rubber wheels; he savoured it, every sound and motion connected with an automobile, a low, heavy automobile.

Stopping directly in front of him, the attendant got out and held open the car door. Dr Eichner studied his face keenly for an instant. He was evidently new at the Clinic's garage.

'Good morning,' said the Doctor.

'Morning, Doc,' the attendant said, 'swell car you got there.' It was a Delahaye, 235.

Dr Eichner came down the steps slowly. 'This is interesting,' he said, 'my experience had given me to believe that the majority didn't care for foreign cars.'

The attendant scratched his head confusedly. 'Well,

Doctor, I been a mechanic for twelve years. Before that I was a trucker. I ought to know a good motor and body when I see it.' He gave the nearest tyre a proving kick with his toe.

'Yes, it's a fine car,' said Dr Eichner getting into it. The door shut with a quiet expensive click, and the attendant stepped back, as though now it were he who held a signal to send the car and driver shooting away.

'Well, so long, Doc,' he said, saluting.

'Yes, so long,' said Dr Eichner with a little smile for him.

Going down the drive, the Delahaye slid through the gravel like a speedboat over a slow swell. The Doctor drove extremely fast.

At the bottom, where the drive poured into Wilshire Boulevard, the car slowed, perceptibly nosing down, and in a sudden squelch-sounding lurch, swerved up and out toward Santa Monica. As the car steadied and settled in the far lane, picking up speed the while, Dr Eichner leaned forward and switched on the radio. It was the hourly news. He pushed the buttons, seven in all, then toyed with the dial-knob, allowing the indicator to rest on a serialized drama as he, sounding the air-horns, took the wheel in both hands and pulled to the left, even into the oncoming speed-lane, to pass a fast moving convertible. Slowing at the intersection, the Doctor turned left into Highlord's Canyon Drive. Ahead, the six-lane stretch tipped and fell in straight and desolate long-graded runs as far as the eye could see. From his breast coat pocket the Doctor drew out a thin silver cigarette case, steadily lowering the throttle while the countryside fled past like fast on the right.

These canyon roads towards noon are blazed with heat, and now the sun lay afire on the mountain land, striking every light surface with wild refraction. Dr Eichner turned down the green glass visor and floored the throttle, racing up a long slow rise in the highway road. The Delahaye touched the crest of the hill with a whirlwind drone and plunged into the descent as for an instant the black sedan was lost behind.

At the far bottom of the hill below was a crossroads with traffic signal, and at quarter way on the descent, a white stone marker showed the distance from there to the intersection as one-eighth mile. It was Dr Eichner's habit to time his descent on leaving the crest so as not to pass this stone marker until the warning amber had shown on the traffic light below; and then to race down the hill at full throttle and beat the red. The duration of the amber was five seconds, so that to clear the intersection ahead of the red light, he must do the eighth-mile in an average of ninety.

Now, as the light was green, he slowed the car leaving the crest approaching the stone marker, and the black sedan swung again into the rear view mirror just clearing the rise behind, very fast. The front wheels of the Delahaye were squarely aline the stone marker, the speedometer at sixty-five, when the amber went on the light below. Flat-mashing the pedal into the foam rubber mat, the Doctor peered keenly ahead, where for the eighth-mile the road fell like an unwound ribbon only rising briefly again past the exact bisection of the crossroad, and the whole, in this perspective, resembled nothing so much as a giant flat cross of the Greek Orthodox Church. The intersection was deserted but for a truck that stood on the right waiting against the light.

In a high, singing speed, the Delahaye lay close to the earth, the tyres sucked and clawed the concrete surface as the car dropped across the hill like a whining shell.

Behind the wheel, slumped British racing style, the Doctor's eyes were just at the level of the top of the steering wheel when his wrists went suddenly stiff and he raised himself looking intently ahead as the large truck below appeared to have made an almost indistinct motion forward. He sounded the horns in two long blasts and at the same moment glanced into the rear view mirror. The left half mirror showed the Doctor's own brow go darkly knit while the other half held the black sedan, moving like a locomotive, apparently intending to pass on the right. In less than a second the two cars were plummeting abreast, and ahead the giant truck began to pull slowly out into the intersection. Dr Eichner exchanged a quick, incredulous look with the two occupants of the other car, a man in front, one in back. The eyes of the driver were fast on the right fender of the Delahaye as he seemed deliberately to edge the black sedan closer alongside with a lead of one or two feet. The man in the rear seat began gesticulating [illegible]

[illegible] at Eichner, and then to glare down the road ahead. But instead of passing, the black sedan maintained the narrow lead, while now, dead ahead of Dr Eichner, loomed the mammoth ten-wheel truck. Between the Doctor's lips, the cigarette butt went suddenly sodden and leached. And as he floored the accelerator, breaking the lead of the sedan, and twisted the wheel convulsedly to the right, the Delahaye slammed twice into the black sedan with a savage ripping noise and the man in the rear was thrown back from the window towards the floor of the car. As he wrenched the wheel to the right again with all his strength, the two cars smashed together, but the Delahaye held its swerve to the right, and before the Doctor the windshield was a shattered haze of grey metal and high wheels where the amber light danced crazily above the scream of burning rubber and a sharp, double-crack as the left fender of the Doctor's car clipped in clearing the great truck just below the tail-gate. Now wide to his right, as Dr Eichner fought the wheel, the black sedan careened out insanely, almost turning over in mid-air until it levelled straight for an instant at blinding speed on the shoulder of the road, and twenty yards past the amber light, with a wild exploding sound, ploughed squarely into a steel telegraph pole.

The Doctor slowed the Delahaye as straight and cautiously reining a mad horse, he brought the car to a stop far down the road. But behind him, fused into the terrible pole, the pinioned twist of sedan belched one oily billow of smoke and burst into fire.

The truck still sat in the intersection, while out halfway between the truck and the wreck, face down in the middle of the highway, was the dark clothed body of a man. Turned in his seat, the Doctor's eye cut a line from the pivotal truck to the burning sedan, traced straight through the outstretched man, cutting dead from the centre of the cross-road — yet at an angle, as the isolate instance, the stunned pendulum swing, never caught at keel but on the rise or fall — for the black burning wreck had torn half its own length up the pole, and the front wheels jutted starkly from either side the vertically split chassis: so thus the wreck itself cast against the sun a smoky crucifixion.

Dr Eichner tried to turn the car around but could get no more than quarter-wheel steering. He began to back up toward the intersection. Behind him then the cab doors of the truck sprang open and a man and woman were down, running toward the body in the highway. They lifted him, as Dr Eichner sounded his horn. 'STOP!' *he* shouted. And while the two carried the loose figure toward the truck, the Doctor tried to increase his speed in reverse but the wheels so rasped against the bent fenders that the car could not be steered. Stopping the car, he jumped out and began to run. Yet, even before he was abreast the burning wreck, a crackling inferno of upholstery and bakelite, impossible to approach, even then the

Truck: 10 wheel, grey, van type with high short cab. No rear licence or markings otherwise.

He touched the pencil to his nose, staring in the direction of the departed truck, then he added :

G.M.? Mack?

and continuing :

Man: stocky build; florid; sandy hair. Brown leather jacket over dark, heavy (possibly corduroy) trousers. Woman: medium dark, straight short hair . . . nondescript dress.

Dr Eichner looked at his wrist watch and, at the top of the page, he wrote :

Drexal and Lord's Canyon Drive. 11.20 - 11.25.

Then he turned, quickly putting away his book, toward the sedan, that blazing wreck, fiery-moated now, where for several feet on either side, the earth itself leapt alight with gas and oil. There was a certain defiance in the way this car burned, and a threat. It was an amalgam of separate parts, no longer distinct, impaled, a fusion. An inviolate pyre.

The sides of the highway were shouldered with fine,

loose gravel, and from a distance behind, Dr Eichner scooped handfuls at the flames. After a futile moment of this he took off his coat and stepped down the rocky culvert aside the road, and up again over a barbed wire fence into the adjacent field. Here, under his knees he spread the coat, forcing it flat against all stick-shoots of weed and nettle, kneeling, as with his hands he began to dig into the dry clay ground, piling what he could onto the coat.

In this attitude, the Doctor started up at the sound of a plane passing far overhead. And caught like this, having only begun to dig, his head cocked to a new, breaking sound, the high distant shrill of an approaching police car: and without standing, as if at last really somehow caught between the siren and the plane, the Doctor knelt, and kneeling, cocked his head from side to side to determine the direction of the sound, the siren.

Then it appeared, the dark patrol car, frozen for an instant at the far top of the hill where last the truck was seen, and it dropped toward the Doctor, the siren suddenly a wailing shriek. Dr Eichner picked up the coat, waved it, running toward the fence and the wreck, as the patrol car hit the intersection in a screaming two-wheel turn and plunged sideways to a sliding stop a few yards behind the burning sedan. Before the dust had cleared, one of the men was out of the car plying the spray of a hand-extinguisher over the wreck. As he stooped through the fence. Dr Eichner shouted to make himself heard above the unchecked siren.

'Did you pass a grey truck?' he cried.

He bounded down the culvert, clutching the coat close, his head straight, as his eyes cast about at the rocky footing. H

to give it

and then with a heavy breath, stepped back and loosened his collar, drew out a great white handkerchief and mopped his face and neck.

The patrolman opened the door of the car and slowly got out, all the while eyeing the burning wreck, where the other officer raced to and fro, pumping the extinguisher viciously. The thin spray of the hand-extinguisher hardly reached the front part of the upright sedan where the flames burned brightest on the blackened pole. Then he turned to the Doctor.

'You see the accident, Mac?'

The Doctor breathed with difficulty from his run back to the road and the shouting against the siren. But at the question he had to smile, rocked forward slightly, his hands clasped over the coat folded against him.

'Yes indeed,' he said, 'I might even say . . .'

'What's your name?' asked the other, already writing.

'Eichner,' said the Doctor shortly. 'There was another vehicle involved in this, a truck. You may have passed it on Drexal, a large grey van.' He intoned the last as a question while the patrolman waited, poised above the pad.

Then, 'STOCK!' They both looked up, surprised almost to anger, as the one with the extinguisher appeared beyond the hood, shouting: 'STOCK! HEY, STOCK!' He was smudged and dishevelled.

'Get emergency,' he said. He spoke with a slight lisp. 'They've got to get a foam-pump out here. Did you see this thing?' He gestured impatiently toward the burning wreck. Patrolman Stockton and the Doctor considered him mutely for a moment, as if the lisp must dry away from the words one by one and let them drop in the dust at his feet all raw and revealed.

'Okay,' muttered Stockton, finally turning away. 'Okay, don't get your crap hot.' He got back into the front seat, lying half across it, to flip one or two switches and speak a hoarse whisper into a microphone attached to the far side of the dash.

Dr Eichner had his memo-book out, open to the page where he had written about the accident, himself leaning through the open door.

'About the truck,' he said softly, nudging Stockton's leg.

The message to the station was incredibly brief, composed of numbers, location, and time. The patrolman flipped the switch again, and sitting up, looked curiously at the Doctor. Then he raised a forefinger near to his right eye and worked it as if calling a small child for a secret. Dr Eichner leaned closer. The patrolman tapped his finger very lightly on the Doctor's shirt front.

'I'll tell you what,' he said, 'you just let us take care of this in our own little way. Okay, fellah?' And giving the Doctor a wink that made him slowly back away, he got out of the car, took the report pad from where he had hooked it onto his belt, and began writing. 'How about that name again?' he said.

allegiance.

'I *think* I begin to understand,' he said. 'You already *have* the truck. Of course. Who else could have reported the accident?' The Doctor spoke the last word on the verge of delight. He pointed a finger at Patrolman Stockton, accusing without malice, but on the contrary, admiringly, as had the officer really been guilty of some laudible mischief.

Officer Stockton read aloud, 'DOCTOR FREDERICK L. EICHNER,' and copied it onto his pad.

The Doctor had been holding his coat. Now he slipped it on and adjusted his tie. 'I'm at Hauptman Clinic,' he said.

The other nodded, turning the card several times in his hand. Then, he looked up, and quite suddenly was staring past the Doctor, down the highway where the Delahaye sat off the road. Though the two men were standing half faced away from the damaged side of the car, it could be seen that the car's wheel alignment was out badly, the body leaning slightly to the left.

'That your car?' The patrolman squinted and stepped off at once in the direction of the Delahaye. Dr Eichner immediately fell in closing step behind, but halfway to the Delahaye, Stockton began to trot, so that when the Doctor reached the car, the patrolman had surveyed it once around and was now down, bent over low, looking at the underside. He rose dusting his hands and rested them against his hips. Facing the Doctor before speaking, he jerked his head solemnly at the damaged side of the Delahaye.

'Your car?'

Dr Eichner was slow to reply.

'Took quite a beating, didn't it?' he said finally, pretending to examine the damage anew.

The other eyed him shrewdly, then without moving his body, turned his head and called over his shoulder to the one at the wreck, he having exhausted the extinguisher, simply standing aside now, watching it burn.

'EDDY! HEY, EDDY!' called Stockton. Eddy came at a brisk gait, his head high in ready interest.

'Take a look at this,' said Stockton jerking again toward the Delahaye.

Slowly walking the length of the car, Eddy gave a long low whistle, at the same time scratching his head.

'You involved in the accident, fellah?' he spoke to Eichner with almost no trace of his former lisp.

The Doctor regarded him incredulously. 'Certainly,' he snapped, 'just as I've been trying to tell this young man,' looking at Stockton who was busy at the pad. 'Now what I want to know,' he went on to Eddy, 'is: who reported the accident? Do you have the truck or not?'

'*Yes* or *no* will do it, Jack,' Stockton said in an off-hand threat from the pad.

Dr Eichner wheeled on him. 'You listen to me, Officer,' he pointed to the burning sedan, 'one man is dead in that sedan, and another in the truck possibly dying, certainly and responsible to the public. And I advise you to keep this in mind.' He ended with a sweep of a shaking finger to include them both, but only Eddy stood impressed, wide-eyed now, while Stockton went on writing and looking up and down the ripped half of the Delahaye.

'Take it easy, fellah,' said Eddy in real concern. And standing close, he actually stroked the Doctor's shoulder. 'We're on the job, you don't have to worry about that, huh, Stock, you tell him.' He smiled a little embarrassedly at his colleague who, whether in feint or truth, was too occupied to take a part. On the pad, Stockton's pencil made a flourish suggesting that a certain phase of the report was at that point definitely complete.

'All right, Doctor,' he said to show his readiness, 'you just tell us now in your own words how the accident happened.'

While the two officers leaned against the side of the Delahaye, the one writing and examining the car continuously, the other following the narrative with open wonder, Dr Eichner stood before them and told exactly what had happened, only omitting the fact of having raced against the red light.

At the end, the officer, Eddy, was agape, as though still waiting for the punch-line, and Dr Eichner had to shrug to show it was all over; so the other could give a long, low whistle and kick his foot in the gravel.

Stockton cleared his throat.

'Where do you *work,* Doctor?' he asked evenly. 'That is, just where is your practice at?'

CHAPTER IV

WHEN Eleanor Thorne returned to the clinic, she found Babs lying on a couch in Nurse's Lounge with a cold compress across her head. They had lost the patient in 28.

It was the first death at the Clinic in more than a month, yet it was the first death where Nurse Mintner had been in direct attendance, for it was she who had injected the coagulants — which had failed to take — and the patient, an extremely old man, had literally died in her arms.

After it was all over, Miss Mintner had come into the rest-room to clean her shoes and change her soiled habit and stockings — so much once toward the end had the old man bled from his nose and mouth.

But, at last, while taking off the ruin of her pure habit, at the close stretched shell of it all broken soft now, and black blood red, even as gutter-razed the white frozen rose, she had become genuinely faint and laid herself down there on the mohair couch in Nurse's Lounge. Later, Beth Jackson came to draw a sheet around her double, [illegible] a danger of it all slipping down across her eyes and nose.

Nurse Thorne stood quiet by the couch, waiting, it would seem, simply to put her hand on Bab's shoulder, she who fluttered a little under the touch, like a waking butterfly, then turned her eyes soft at Eleanor Thorne. 'We lost 28,' she said and sobbed pitifully till the instant her eyes went great with the hopeless and overwhelming wonder of it, and her face moved slowly away into the pillow. 'Oh why?' she begged. 'Why? *Why?*'

Eleanor pressed at the bare shoulder gently. 'Please,' she said in a firm voice. 'Please.'

But grimacing, Miss Mintner knotted her tiny fist and struck it softly against the pillow. *'Why?'* she demanded, resolute but still tearful.

Nurse Thorne sat down on the edge of the couch, gradually massaging Barbara's shoulder. 'Please—please don't Barbara.' And it was the first time she had called Miss Mintner by her given name. 'He was very old,' she added in real sympathy, fingering the tracery of near lace at her shoulder—the way the young girl was lying, twisted on the couch, the strap could have seemed to be cutting the circulation from her left arm.

Miss Mintner slowly brought herself around to face Nurse Thorne. 'If only *you'd* been here,' and at the point her voice filled with tribute there was the slightest reproach in her eyes.

'I know, dear,' said Eleanor turning her look abstractly to where her own fingers kneaded beneath the binding filigree. 'I was held up at Bullock's.'

Precisely then, on a chance glance at the window past Nurse Thorne, Babs Mintner gave a small start, raising one hand to her mouth, but as quickly uncovering a brave smile and one bare shoulder for Garcia, he who was standing there on the terrace, looking in.

'What on earth!' cried Eleanor Thorne, following her. She sailed to the window, shouting. 'Garcia!' exactly as if she had expected him to turn and run, run from where she hovered above him, actually speechless for the moment, as he frowning what under these circumstances could have been certain disapproval, stood quite still. Then she managed such outrage for him, hands on her hips, the accusation so glaring it might sear straight through his breast, burning past the heart of every last furtive mangled-tongue degenerate crouched, small matter how deep, in his rat-hole of lying guilt.

'What IS this, Garcia! What are you DOING there!'

But the gardener stared imperturbably past her to Babs Mintner, lying on the couch, smiling through tears.

'Well, I have never!' said Nurse Thorne placing herself squarely before him so he could not see beyond.

'You, Garcia! What does this mean?'

'It's for her,' said the gardener, obviously disturbed by the effort of speaking in English. He tried to look past Nurse Thorne by moving his head to the left and right, stepping forward and back, careful at the same time not to

'You want to *see* him?' put in Nurse Thorne, incredulous. '*Now?* You don't mean you want to see him *now!*'

'*Why*, how do you mean?' said Babs, seeming really ingenuous.

'But what on earth for?' the other demanded, freshly irate, actually blocking her way.

'It's all right,' repeated Babs, weakly, as if she might faint. 'It will only take a minute.'

'Well for heaven's sake put on your whites!'

Eleanor Thorne took the fresh habit from the chair and helped her into it.

And Babs agreed wearily, romantically, as if the sweat and tears of twelve-hour bombardments had made the young nurse *forget* for a moment that she was a woman, beautiful and desired.

So when the top button was done and the girl safely belted, Eleanor Thorne wheeled and left the room in a huff.

'I'll be having a word with your superiors soon,' Dr Eichner was saying to Stockton and Eddy from the back seat of the patrol car *en route* to the station. 'In light of that, perhaps you can realize it might be advantageous to you now to answer the question I put earlier: *who reported this accident?*'

The two sat mute-skulled before him, Stockton drowned sullen and square-shouldered at the wheel, while Eddy, by the window, was propped so straight and stiff-kneed he could have just been handed a crumpet in the Commissioner's living room.

The Doctor went on, half patiently, 'Since you obviously failed to get the truck . . .'

'Why don't you tell the Doctor who reported it?' Stockton broke in to Eddy, who began to move himself then, gradually, to face the Dr Eichner.

'Ain't nobody reported it, Doc,' he said, turning completely around. 'We seen the smoke.'

Nurse Thorne went straight to her office, strictly stepping the distance, her close locked lips like the shutting edge of a knife. Once inside her door she half opened it in closing her eyes and, folding slightly at the shoulders, pressed back against the door as it gradually closed behind her both hands clutching the knob tight to a white-edged rose: but she was not alone. Beth Jackson — at the seaward window, moored as some great used ship, or listless bulk which moved in sighs — swayed at the ocean window, while all around her dark bunned head frayed a vigorous silver. She was the most unkempt woman in the Clinic.

'Oh, there you are, Beth,' Eleanor Thorne improvised, going to the desk and taking up some papers.

'It's about that shipment of crocks,' said Beth, not to be taken in.

It was almost a month now that a hospital supply salesman, in failing to find Nurse Thorne had called on Beth Jackson:

drawn against the day, and lights turned up — these lights, as hidden tubes which dealt from nowhere every corner with gentle searching light, did almost as sunlight passing paper screens faintly tinted blue : and the illusion of permitting no shadow gave a soft uncertain swiftness to the room.

The young man sat with his hands, which seemed not to move unnecessarily, turned palms up, gathering, as it were, calm from the air; and the effect of this was the evident strength of stillness in his face and shoulders. Apparently he represented an unknown house, one with which the Clinic had never taken account.

Beth Jackson had given him a cup of hot coffee, with a dram or so medicinal rum in it, and had drawn off one for herself as she bade the young man sit to dry before an electric heater of the large, reflector type. In only a seersucker suit he was soaked to the skin, and when he half rose to hand her the catalogue, his smile at last breaking the stillness as though it were a book of comics for a grown child he handed her, his forward foot on the marble floor made a swamp-step squish that caused Beth Jackson to close the book on the very place he had opened it.

'Gracious that won't do,' she cried, and was up to fetch a heavy towel from an open cupboard near. 'Now give them a good rub,' she, at her most bluff humour, 'or else you'll be staying on here as a *patient* !'

She sat down opposite, bent forward for the moment with

her outstretched fingers in touching adjustments to the spanning tilt of red copper between them, properly set as now to mirror and cup the glittered heat in a swirl at its centre-source where it cast edgewise out in diffusion one flat, elemental image of the burning coils, which were yet, themselves, as the source, small, diversely-sized, and of a wire-like complexity.

'Dr Hauptman will have him one salesman less, and one patient more!' she revised, jovial now, settling in comfort with the balanced phrase which, too, may have represented a joke, since Dr Hauptman had been dead for years. This was something the young man could not have known, though he did smile with her now, and shyly enough to encourage her bluff.

'Oh yes, it's very funny, isn't it?' as she pretended to admonish him, while not wanting anything really ever to be other than funny between them. 'It's all very funny to you young people while you've got your health, but wait till the doctor starts dropping by twice an hour with a needle for you then you change your tune, believe me, I've seen it too often.' And her dart-round eyes, caught up as they were in the wide day-grey of his own, narrowed to serious as she finished, thinking certainly of treatments given there in her own department.

'Doctor Hauptman, you mean?' said the young man, more than half in his innocence.

And this had almost floored her. Yet, first it simply set her agape, aback the flat moon face as clawed by one terribly thin lightning frown, caught for the instant stark between two lights. But the good faith of the young man was above question, so then she just broke up, laughing.

It began, this laugh, as one of those laughs that are real: rumbling down in the pit of herself — as if where swarmed on the chair in the farthest tips of her person and back again, its bulk-shuddering reverberations.

'Dr Hauptman and his needle,' said the young man, playing it out, hiding his face in feigned alarm. 'Look out!'

'Yes, yes,' she cried, breathless, giving up, waving him off with her hand. 'Oh yes!' It was too much. 'Dr Hauptman's needle!' she repeated, falsely having heard. 'Yes, oh dear, oh God!'

After a point, however, it was no longer a genuine laugh but some unnerved noise of control as she forcibly seized the rhythm of the laugh and propelled it, in the illusion of riding it out; as if that dead laugh were this same laugh dying; or yet, again, as how past the brief wildness of unreined flats, horses slow and mounted men gain control at last beginning to ride, but do know then, in their heart of hearts, that the race is over. Nor could this sustain but follow the laugh with its nerve ripped out into wiping eyes and the wag of her great grey head.

'Dear, oh dear, oh gracious,' and the scold of her red eyes on him for some indescribable mischief lead into a silence where they both sat easily, he in his blamelessness, she in her inexasperate patience. Yet out of this silence, like the circular rise of a great winged bird : not as a threat but a guidance, swept the dulcet beat of crumpling rain in the hushcloth stucco of the outside wall; and again, even as falsely quick or near on wind-sung darts at the curtained glass.

'Not that we don't have more than we can handle as it is,' she began knowingly, in an effort to be sensible, touching her dishevelled bun, 'with a waiting-list in some departments at that, gracious knows!' And shaking her head twice slowly, she took to the catalogue, but could not resume it wholly until the young man actually leaned over and began really then to remove his shoes.

'Well, now,' she started turning the pages, settling again with deliberate interest and understanding, some dear and unread mother first to hear the long unpublished poem of her son.

'Now these are nice,' she would say, raising with her look a certain acknowledgement for the young man, 'these aluminium Serve-Alls on page 29.' She lowered her voice in sudden confidence, even to half closing the book. 'I'll tell you what: I'm just going to make a note of some of these things, and I'll see Eleanor Thorne the minute she's back!' and before the young man could alter his smile, she had tried to withdraw all but the gesture, reaching out to touch his arm. 'You see now we're with Aldridge and National Hospital, we have been for years. What they don't have they seem to manage for when we need it.' She took her hand from him in a sweep toward the mars-man array of chrome apparatus bearing from the next room. 'These are all Nationals,' she said, turning on her chair, 'except this one,' toward a lone thin case in the room, holding, as it did one silver spider of machine, so intricate and whole as to appear rightly sufficient in itself alone behind the shimmering glass. They looked on it briefly, almost without hope, as if its implications could never be really taken in at all.

'It's a Maidestone,' she said brightly enough, 'an original. Dr Maidestone designed it, and it was set up by Talbots. Dr purchasing,' she said, almost darkly, yet allowed him his smile. 'That was ten years ago.'

Actually it was thirteen years ago, just to that very day, that the Clinic had centralized its buying. Previously, the twelve various departments of the Clinic had received the salesmen, seen their catalogues of ware, and through these salesmen had given their orders — to suppliers who were paid later by the administrator, Mr Rogers, upon presentation of their bills at his office. Then, the departments were in turn responsible for submitting their invoices, and tallying in on their departmental allowances — to Mr Rogers, whose burden, it must be said, was even at that point particularly felt, since the Clinic might have accounts with as many as thirty-seven different firms at once, the invoices continually being forgot or misplaced by the departments, and their allowance overstepped, padded or whatnot — and *especially* felt, since he, Mr Rogers, must report quarterly to the board, a group of public-spirited businessmen who had, in the early days, lent Dr Hauptman a great deal of money. And subsequent to the extension of certain government health programmes, of discount and subsidy, to include such private institutions as this Clinic, the pressure of the board, on Mr Rogers in his confused relationship with departmental spending had caused that poor man's mind, as it was, one evening before the board, being layed open layer by layer, to flip. So that he had to spend two months in a rest-home in Arizona. And it was during his absence that there developed the practice of centralized buying, through a sole agent, which as it happened, was the newly appointed head nurse, Eleanor Thorne. Now the procedure was established that a department would make known its needs by memorandum to Nurse Thorne's office which would first record it against the department's quarterly allowance, then place an order with Aldridge or National Hospital, two of the largest hospital supply houses in the world. The resultant shipment would be received by this same general office, opened, the invoice removed, re-checked on the department's allowance sheet, and finally carried, invoice and package, by Albert, the ward-boy, round to the department concerned, where the invoice, hardly leaving Albert's hand for the purpose, was initialled by that department-head, and delivered on to the administrator, Mr Rogers' office.

This procedure was practice, not policy, since it had never been formally revealed to the board. And while it was yet within the prerogative of individual department-heads to order independently of Nurse Thorne, there had been, of such, only a few, isolated cases during the past 13 years.

'Oh we can do better than that now I'm sure,' Beth Jackson was saying to the young man, for he was only blotting. 'The circulation,' she said indistinctly, and next was on her knees giving his feet and ankles a vigorous rub. When they were quite, possibly painfully, red, she swaddled the heavy towel there and raised her eyes to his own. 'There now!' she exclaimed with too much finality if she were to remain an instant longer on her knees. 'This is pneumonia weather,' she promised in retreat, 'whether you know it or not!'

He nodded, laughing softly out of politeness, he who could have been as young as the boy she had lost in the war. So she half rose, leaving the towel gathered in warmth around his feet, and herself to turn away holding two small socks these socks on the edge of his chair, toward the electric heater, to dry.

What was the most understandable upshot of this interlude was, in the end, Beth Jackson's having placed an order with the young man for six crockery basins for her department. And this shipment had arrived at Nurse Thorne's office. Not as an important package but as one unexpected, opening it became something like the days before centralized buying when opening the packages always held some suspended interest of the surprises at Christmas. But, what with the breach of policy this package represented, Nurse Thorne quite forgot to remove the invoice, or if she did remove it, forgot that she had done so, and above all, where she had put it — for it occurred to her three days later that she had made no entry on the record. It was then, that after considerable effort, she began to recall exactly the scene in part, of Albert holding the open-top, pine board box to his chest, his white face strained beneath grimace as by some stiff tangle of under surface wire, while there, from where his chin touched, or so she recalled, the one, half-exposed crock, rose a curl of excelsior, bunched as it was in almost concealing, twice-folded, the sea-blue square of the invoice. And then he was gone. Actually, what she did recall was the figure,

'10.95,' marked on the remaining half-top of the box in black crayon, and this figure she had entered into the allowance sheet, there, either in contempt or uncertainty, to slur the four ciphers into being very nearly illegible.

'It's about those crocks, El,' Beth Jackson was saying in Nurse Thorne's office.

This might have been a question (*Is* it about those crocks?) from the way Eleanor Thorne chose to answer, simply: 'Yes, it is, Beth,' regarding her quite seriously, holding a patient smile.

'Oh, you've heard then?' asked Beth, assuming that same smile of patience with the other's guilt.

'What I mean is this, Beth : if we take on accounts with houses that don't know our procedure here — though a new house, how we could expect them to is beyond me — then there's bound to be trouble. Do you see my point?'

Whereupon Beth managed a frown. 'Why, how do you mean?' she asked.

'Well here for example, what's your problem over those crocks?'

'Oh, mind I don't say I have one,' replied fat Beth as airily as had they been speaking of lovers, two pretty girls. But even so saying, her mind's-eye picqued with an image of gyno and her own Jane Ward, unpacking, as had happened, in Beth's absence, the box of crocks, excitedly stuffing excelsior down the incinerator-shaft, and along with it, perhaps, the precious fold of invoice. They had never been sure. 'The fact is, El, Mr Rogers asked me to look into it.'

'Your Jane? Jane Ward? She was there then?'

'Jane, the poor mopsy! You know what a stickler she is for procedure — "red-tape" I called it to her — I can tell you she was almost in tears. "Now you're to listen," I told her, "it isn't our worry I can tell you for sure! We're here to see to the women, and not for signing scraps and bits of paper every time you turn around! What they want to do about that is nobody's affair but their own. And that's what they're paid for!" After twenty-eight years I ought to know what my duties are, Eleanor, I told her exactly that!' For this was nine years more than Nurse Thorne could say.

'How was the shipment unpacked, Beth? That may be the answer.'

'Well, of course, it's a shame I wasn't there when it did come, though mind I don't say it would have made a difference in the conditions.'

'No?'

'Oh no, I was at Hillcrest with Dr Stevens! I thought you knew.'

'Yes, I see.'

'I mean it *was* my day for Hillcrest, you would have known that.'

'Of course. Then it *was* Jane Ward unpacked the shipment?'

'Jane was in a state when I got there. I shouldn't want this to go any further than the two of us, El, but I think it's *Albert*. The child's terrified.'

'Ridiculous!'

'Eleanor, I told her exactly that! But then you know yourself. And she is such a mopsy! "Unawakened," I call it. Babs too, the darling.'

Jane Ward was the youngest nurse in the Clinic, was, in fact one full year the junior of Babs Mintner, though Babs was the prettier by far.

'Beth, that *is* ridiculous,' repeated Eleanor cautiously, rather pleased.

Beth lowered her voice. 'Yes, you mind I'm not blaming Albert, gracious knows, poor devil, he does his job. And El, when I think what must go through that mind of his!'

'Yes,' mused Eleanor, 'I suppose.'

'Still in all, we have got the girls to think of now, El, especially Janie and Babs.'

'Barbara? What has she to do with it then?'

'Well, not that exactly. What I mean is, girls at their age, El, you know there's bound to be some complication. And then on top of it a young man popping up in every direction! It's only natural. And Babs I believe especially.'

'But why Barbara?' asked Nurse Thorne evenly.

'It wouldn't be my place to say it, Eleanor, but I simply can't help not feeling that it isn't somehow a mistake putting the youngsters alone like that together so often, especially under the conditions.' And so saying, she actually nodded toward the window, even in the general direction morning, exactly. If you could have seen our Babs! I'll tell you she was on pins and needles the whole time. I don't know when I've seen a youngster so upset!'

'Yes, this *morning,*' said Eleanor, taking a lighter view, 'of course that was unfortunate I admit, Beth, I was held up at Bullock's. But then ask yourself, how often is it to happen at that?'

'Often enough I should say from what I've seen,' returned Beth with dignity.

'What, an intoxication case in the morning? Really, Beth,' said Eleanor with a strange laugh, 'you don't mean it!'

'How's that?' cried Beth, slightly raucous at being so off guard, but just as quick, so knowingly arch as her bulk and her great padded brows could manage, even so as not to be left out entirely, she said in a fine voice: 'And who's been at it this time if I may ask?'

'Why no, Beth, who are you thinking of then, not Mr Edward's boy from the college?'

'Ralph Edwards, of course, Eleanor, who else *would* it be?'

'Well! Yes, well, I couldn't say, of course, there may be something to it at that, Beth, what do you think?'

'I'll tell you what I think, El,' said Beth grandly, 'I think our girls have a crush on the young man. Unless

I'm *very much* mistaken,' she added, as though she almost never were.

'Jane too then?' said Eleanor favouring another subject.

'What else?' asked Beth, as if now at last, they lay, all of them, really helpless before the man.

There followed a pause which seemed to expand with Beth's own growing anticipations, and Eleanor cleared her throat to speak plainly. 'I don't know, Beth. Have you thought about this at all?'

'Why, how do you mean?'

'No. I mean, is there anything you can suggest?'

'Well yes, El,' said Beth, emphatic enough, though clearly she was improvising, 'what I'm wondering now is this: when I've a day at Hillcrest, oughtn't I to take my Jane along? After all, we've got to get in her General sometime, and heavens we could use her, you've no idea!'

When Nurse Thorne agreed to take this up at first opportunity with Dr Charles, head of the Clinic, the two women passed on to the subject of this old man himself and his coming retirement, following which they spoke briefly, and somewhat on the oblique, of his possible successor, seemingly the most likely of which was Dr Eichner, of whom at 49 they said, 'comparatively young,' and as Beth Jackson pointed up, 'on the very threshold of his career.'

There was then no further mention of the crocks as the talk of the women grew vague, themselves drifting apart, toward their own specifics, as in distraction to all the windows' changing light, dying brilliance of the outside day — for whereas had a hundred swift young clouds, un-

[illegible] afternoon, through lassitude, or knew not what to do but lay all huddled now as if almost asleep beneath the sun — and this had filled the western sky with shadow.

At the station, the patrolmen turned in their report and stood together now with Dr Eichner, before the precinct head, Captain Howie 'Dutch' Meyer. After reading the report, from which, time after time, he left off, simply to look up at the accused Dr Eichner, the Captain, a small, grey man, well past the retirement age, cocked his head and made his eyes start out, as though to crane over beyond his glasses. 'Well, well,' he said — and in this he resembled nothing so much as some veteran film-actor celebrated for his handling of character roles — '*Well, well, well!* How long you been in this country, Mister?' And before the Doctor could reply, if, indeed, he would have to such seeming irrelevance, the Captain, resting on his elbows, raised both hands, palms flat together, before his face which was set with a patronizing, almost brotherly smile, and spoke the Doctor's name, greatly exaggerating the guttural of it: 'EICHNER,' and continued in a bored, flat voice where he tried to nail each word with irritation and amusement. 'What are you, Doctor? Dutch or German-Jew?'

An ill-bred man, this Captain delighted in handling the cases of first generation immigrants.

Dr Eichner stood easily, cleared his throat once, and when it was quite apparent that they were all waiting for him to speak, addressed the Captain. 'Identify yourself, please.'

'How's that?' said Captain Meyer, though he had heard very well.

'I'm asking you to identify yourself, Captain. I think I'm entitled to know who it is I'm speaking with, isn't that so?' He addressed the last to the patrolman, Eddy, without lowering his voice even though they were standing shoulder to shoulder, whereupon Eddy grimaced uneasily, shifted from one foot to the other, and failed to meet the Doctor's eye, but where his allegiance now lay was never more uncertain. 'You'll find it in your ordinances, I believe,' the Doctor ended sternly, nodding his head.

'Captain Meyer,' said the old man distinctly then, '—or so I'm told, Doctor, though you might be better informed about it. Captain Howard K. Meyer, Middletown, Pennsylvania. Police Officer Number 4276, County of Los Angeles. If you'd like to see my record,' he went on, shaming some famous old actor or other in a joke, with a wink at the two patrolmen, '—though I won't say it's exactly "light-reading." Forty-two years' worth to be exact, Doctor!'

'That won't be necessary,' said Dr Eichner shortly. 'Let's just get on with the accident report.'

'Accident?' returned the Captain. He allowed himself still another reflective look at the report in his hands, shaking it a little. 'Could be, Doctor, *could* be. But from

habit, to focus her eyes there.

Sometimes, alone here in Nurses Rest Rooms, the girl would enjoy the most elusively delicious, and somehow unexpected transports of fantasy. These were not exactly vicarious, since they did not seem, really to concern *her,* even indirectly, but dealt rather with the reflection in the mirror which she had to glance at from time to time as if to assure herself that the adventure was real after all. Today, however, for some reason or other, Barbara found the images too fragmentary, the sequences broken and unsatisfactory, or more precisely, *unfair*; so that after a few minutes she got up and sat at the dressing-table where she began to brush her hair, which she appeared to do with an infinite concern and tenderness, though actually she was absorbed in counting: twenty-five strokes each, to back and sides. Having no head for figures, she was very careful. Then she combed it and, finally, fluffed it here and there with her hand, setting to rights a temple-ringlet or two. She put on fresh lipstick and squeezed two blackheads from her nose which she dusted then with very light powder. She believed that she was mostly appreciated for her fresh, natural look — which was, in a sense, true. Then at last she stood, and still before the glass where her eyes now were less adoring than critical, adroitly smoothed the back of the skirt which was slightly wrinkled from lying with it so drawn under. She adjusted her habit completely, from collar and shoulders to the hem — first, frontally before the glass; then sideways, at which time, it still being before lunch, she drew in her belt one notch. That she was able to do this, had anyone else been present, would have come to her as an animated walked about the room with an easy, inimitable assurance, holding the coke which was only half-finished and, by now, quite flat.

A perfect white at the window, looking over the broad estate, the slopes of green and the planes of white cement, with her head lowered in absently sipping the coke, and her eyes raised round and wide, almost as in magic goodness, she could have been the one child-princess of an angel-cake kingdom, all white-iced and perfect. She was standing slightly back from the window, with the same cautious ease she had crossed the room, now in avoiding the everplay of Pacific breeze which stirred over the land with an anxiety that never left off lightness. So, back from the window and distrait, Babs was not aware of the car's approach until it was there, rounding the gravel slope before her. It was a yellow convertible, and the girl's first impression was that the occupants were movie-stars, since they both wore dark glasses, and the young woman at the wheel had her startling sun-like hair half hidden in a jet black kerchief, while her face shown brown as fine leather. She stopped the car at the Clinic door, and the young man got out, handsome and worldly, his dress, it appeared, richly casual. When he turned his back to close the car door and speak a word to his companion who raised her hand briefly and smiled before pulling away,

Babs believed for an instant that he was Tyrone Power, and a drop or two melted from her heart. In the next moment the young man, having apparently seen Barbara at the window when he turned to bound up the Clinic steps, slowed his pace and, looking that way, was waving and smiling, unmistakably at her. And it was only then, of course, that she realized, though not without a shocking ambivalence that ricocheted between discovery and insult that it was Mr Edwards the pharmacist's nephew, Ralph, from the University. And she saw too clearly now that what had been his weary, decadent smile, was, after all, simply a boyish grin. She wanted to be furious with him for this, and for the moment, almost was, for where her mouth had dropped slightly open when he first waved, she snapped it shut now and twisted away with a really offended toss of her head, as though he had again, for the second time in as many days, tried to look up her dress.

CHAPTER VI

BABS MINTNER owned a pair of sun-glasses, but she never wore them except when she went swimming, which she occasionally did on Saturday afternoon, when she was off duty from the Clinic. To wear them otherwise, not being a movie-star, she would have felt too self-conscious, or even 'silly.' And though the glare of the sun could be troublesome during her lunch time away from the

Once she had taken a de luxe tour of Hollywood which included having lunch at the Brown Derby, and the most impressive thing she had yet seen in her life was, in that already tomb-grey, the dark and isolate forms hunched silently over strange plates, and so sinister behind their smoked glass that the poor girl had failed to recognize a single soul.

'That is the famous director, Bunuel,' the guide had said of one serious man who sat alone to eat and drink without once raising his eyes past a pair of glasses that were death black; and for a long time afterwards Babs had felt, at the movies, an anticipation over the screen-credits, looking for the name, Bunuel. Later she began to regret that it had not been Hitchcock, or Cecil B. De Mille, she had seen at the Brown Derby. But she had never even for a moment, doubted the dangerous importance of the men in black glasses, nor above all, their right to wear them.

So, standing at the Dispensary counter and seeing that Ralph Edwards, even now, had his dark glasses on, made her so cross she could have snatched them away and pinched his nose.

'Hello,' he said, almost absently. He was just hanging up his jacket, although it had been fully ten minutes since

Babs saw him enter the Clinic. And having taken this tack, he forced her into changing her lines completely, though, even so, they had only been half-planned.

'Oh, hello,' she said coolly, even as if she hadn't expected to see him here, nor, certainly, could care less.

For some reason this caused him to laugh, and when he came to the counter he was all boyish again and smiling. Below the dark glasses, his teeth were like pieces of bevelled ivory. They were so straight and even they looked false, and the awareness that they were actually alive came as a very disturbing threat to the girl.

'Where is Mr Edwards?' she said, trying to recover, looking around the hall and then at her watch, which, without even having made it out, she began to wind, so tight that it almost burst then and there.

'The pharmacist,' she added quickly, in a tone which would make it certain she did not wish a repetition of the young man's last performance.

'Do you like music?' he asked, undeceived, and suddenly bold in a matter-of-fact voice, still smiling, his head to one side. And he reached in his shirt pocket to take out what might have been two tickets to a school concert. But the *truth* was, that ever since his unexpected laugh, displeasure on the girl's face had grown so fiercely that now, when she raised her head, she was so obviously near to tearful outrage that he hesitated, and asked, in real sympathy: 'What's the matter?' Whereas Babs, perhaps mistaking, or rightly taking, this for pity, said furiously, straight at where his eyes lay smoked in mystery behind the offensive glass, 'Nothing's the matter with ME! What's the matter with YOU?' And so saying, she turned [illegible] blonde who still smiled easily from behind the cream-coloured wheel of the yellow convertible.

CHAPTER VII

THE new Los Angeles County Records Building was constructed after a design by Raoul Krishna, which the artist made in 1936, when he was living in Salt Lake City. The original blueprint had been drawn up and entered for competition at the Texas Centennial, where, had it been placed, it would have become one of the permanent exposition buildings of the State Park Fair Grounds in Dallas. With its failure there, however, the artist revised the drawing, and where the main façade had originally been fashioned to meet the requirements of opening in wide descent onto the State Park Esplanade, introduced, instead, a level, domed cloister with eight converging approaches. And in this form, the plan was submitted, during the next few years, to various competitions in the United States and Europe, occasionally receiving some secondary acclaim. In 1940, it came to the attention of the first woman member of the Los Angeles Board of City Planning. An extremely active and popular person, the wife of an influential citizen, she was herself a patron of the arts and, in fact, so much so of this particular artist that she presented his plan to the Board. It was accepted in the summer of 1940 and, following one major alteration (where the original had called for a gigantic, self-supporting dome-roof — which, because of the earth tremors in the Los Angeles area, was held inadvisable — a more conventional type roof-structure was submitted) the work was begun, and the building completed on Christmas Eve Day of that year. It was an immense structure, made almost entirely of plaster-stone, and at a cost of about two million dollars.

Dr Eichner scarcely knew this building. Although he had passed it in his automobile a number of times, and, from being well-read, knew its history, civic functions and so forth, it was his habit to give almost no visual attention to things which were not immediately and vitally pertinent. Yet, it must be said, that once a thing did become pertinent, he had an amazing faculty for absorbing it wholly. A case in point was his behaviour toward Music. When he went to the opera, for example, it was not without having first made himself closely familiar with the life of the composer and, so far as possible, the principal singers. And while he had no particular taste for music or drama, during the presentation he scrupulously followed a libretto and score, the margins of which he filled with comments about the performance, always in the language of its presentation. For this purpose, he had once learned Italian in six hours.

papers,
legal journals; devouring everything that might in any way relate to the situation.

Before the evening was out, he had even familiarized himself with a plan of the County Records Building, and now, as he stood outside it, shading his eyes, at 10.20, precisely ten minutes before the scheduled convening of the Jury, he surveyed the whole with interest, mentally checking the accuracy of the detailed description he had previously read. Standing close, the building was a formless stretch of flat plastered white, without depth or surface quality except at the farthest end where one brief section was flung so abruptly against the sky it seemed to die away entirely, leaving only a texture, a sick glaze in the heat of noon. More than anything else the modern building resembled a huge uncertain mausoleum.

In five minutes the Doctor walked half the frontal length of the building, retraced his steps to the cloistered dome and entered the main door, past which he was inside a great, octagonal, reception room. The temperature here, like that in an air-conditioned cinema, was immediately refreshing. High above were countless thin panels of frosted skylight, meeting ice-white walls and, below the floor of green slate, an effect given point at the great room's centre by the location there of a booth structure, also octagonal, marked on each side *Information*, and made entirely of aluminium. Standing just inside the door, the Doctor examined the room at length. The surrounding walls held numbered glass doors, three to each of the eight sides, leading, as Dr Eichner knew, to the various chambers of law, opening and closing in both directions, soundlessly.

Having digested the scene, he went directly, as planned, to the Information Booth and, without a word, presented his convocation. The booth was occupied by a pale old man in a seersucker suit who was reading a pocket-book held flat before him on the metal counter. The old man looked first at the convocation, then at the Doctor with an air of annoyance, perhaps for his speechlessness since he in turn kept an exaggerated silence and, returning the convocation, simply pointed to a directional indicator, near one of the doors, marked, like the convocation, '16th District, 8th Sessions.' Dr Eichner had not expected these directional indicators, apparently a recent innovation, as they had not been mentioned in the description of the building; so, for the moment, he was taken aback.

'Good!' he said then, receiving the convocation in his hand again and starting to leave; but he stopped short, as on an afterthought, and spoke out amiably to the old man who had already gone back to his book.

'This is Judge Fisher's Session, isn't it?'

'Judge Thornton Fisher?' said the other, raising his thin grey head. He looked at the Doctor cagily, as though suspecting a trap, and shook his head, a slow wag with eyes closed. 'Not Judge Fisher,' he said flatly, but continued at once in a forgiving tone, 'Judge Fisher is not here any more.' Unmistakably, there was finality and an irritating was so genuine that the old man realized then he wasn't being baited after all, and so, even closed the book to make the most of it, leaning forward across the aluminium, his white face livid now in sudden and almost obscene confidence.

'Well, he's dead,' he said in a soft whining effort to get some of the Doctor's sympathy himself, and so saying, half-satisfied, sat back stiffly to hold his book in readiness and continue as matter-of-fact: 'Day before yesterday. Or maybe it was Wednesday; it *was* Wednesday. Asphyxiation by carbon monoxide . . .'

'Well, wasn't public notice given?' asked the Doctor, impatient now that time was growing short.

'It was in the *papers*,' replied the old man, frowning fixedly at the Doctor; and then suddenly, as though on pure impulse, he reached in his pocket and drew out a flat, limp-worn billfold. His movement was abrupt, but, once the bill-fold was out, he opened it with slow effort and, even more laboriously, unfolded the newspaper clipping he took from inside, at last spreading it flat on the counter before them both. The banner read:

'TRAGEDY IN WOODLAWN'

and beneath:

'Custom Cadillac Is
His Death-Chamber'

'I know this banner,' said Dr Eichner, almost challengingly. 'There's no indication here that . . .' He broke off then with a show of impatience and read the item in its entirety. It began : 'Thornton K. Fisher, prominent civic leader and judge, resident of the fashionable Woodlawn district, was found late last evening, dead of asphyxiation, in his automobile.' The item continued at some length, describing the circumstances of the tragedy, the discovery of the body, and so on, concluding : 'Friends and relations knew of no reason why Judge Fisher would have wanted to take his own life.'

Dr Eichner did not ordinarily read the newspapers, preferring rather to get the news in weekly retrospect, from the periodicals—for these organs treated events of a preceding week as an understandable sequence, and gave them discernible pattern. On the previous evening, however, in preparing for the hearing, he had scanned the last week's daily papers, so as to be up to date. Apparently, the ambiguous banner for the Fisher tragedy had misled him into overlooking the substance of the item. Even so, he finished reading it now with a snort of contempt and flung the clipping, as though it were actually worthless, to one side. 'Still no indication,' he said emphatically, 'of a change in 8th Sessions ! Who's presiding now ?'

The old man gathered up the clipping ruefully, even ignoring the Doctor, who looked on amazed that the other could still imagine the clipping to be of any use. Suddenly, however, he was evidently so touched by the old man's false scorn that he reached out his hand and laid it gently on his shoulder. 'I beg your pardon,' he said. 'I didn't mean to offend you. It was simply that the coverage in wholeheartedly.

said the Doctor, patting his shoulder. 'I'm very sure of it. And I'm sorry.' Then, after a reasonable pause, he continued, 'I must leave now. I have a Hearing in 8th Sessions.' He looked at his watch; it was 10.35. 'I wonder if you could tell me who's presiding now.'

The old man had taken out his handkerchief and was blowing his nose. 'Judge Lester,' he said indistinctly, and the Doctor, his head back slightly, eyes half closed in an attitude of concentration, recalled a dozen or so other names beginning with *L*. 'Not *Lessing*?' he ventured at last, with a frown to express the doubt of it.

'Judge Lessing? Judge Tom Lessing is in 18th District Criminal Courts,' said the old man indignantly, and immediately appeared to be warming toward the Doctor. 'Judge Howard Lester,' he said, putting his handkerchief away now to sit bright-eyed, white hands folded tight and small.

'I don't know him then,' said the Doctor seriously. 'What are his leanings?'

'How's that?' cried the old man.

'I mean, what is his background?'

'Judge Lester? He's from out of state,' replied the old man expansively, 'Arizona. Tucson, I believe. Tucson, Arizona. Did you say you have a Hearing? Today?'

'Yes. But, just a moment—you say that Judge Lester

is from *Arizona*? Isn't that unusual, that he should be from out of state? This is a County matter, is it not?'

'Not at all!' replied the old man knowingly. 'Not-at-all. Judge Fisher was born in Vienna himself! An American citizen though. His mom and dad were both Americans. His dad—I knew Judge Fisher's daddy—was with the State Department in Vienna. Mark Fisher! A grand old man! Markham R. Fisher.' He ended somewhat lamely, and it was obvious that he had really exaggerated how well he had known the elder Fisher.

'I'm afraid you don't understand,' said Dr Eichner almost coldly. 'What I'm referring to is Judge Lester's *County record*, his past decisions.'

The old man, perhaps only at a loss being told he did not understand, seemed taken aback. Then he tightened his clasped hands and said with a child-like haughtiness, 'I'm afraid we don't give out that type of information.'

Dr Eichner started to speak, but glanced at his watch instead. He was already ten minutes late for the Hearing. 'I believe that's my door there, isn't it?' he asked in a more formal, friendly way, gesturing toward where the other had pointed before.

'That's right. At the end of the hall,' replied the old man gloomily.

'Well, thanks for your trouble,' said the Doctor with a wave of his hand, 'and good morning.'

The other responded with a sulky nod, but as Dr Eichner turned to move away, he called after him warmly: 'It ain't the Judge that matters at a Hearin', it's the Jury!' and he even gave him a smile of hope.

'Yes, of course,' said the Doctor almost without hear-

CHAPTER VIII

WHEN Dr Eichner reached 8th Sessions antechamber, he was more than ten minutes late, and the Hearing had already begun. He was admitted at once by a shabbily uniformed attendant who gave him a strange look as he quietly opened the courtroom door.

Here was a small amphitheatre of the kind in use in most European universities, arranged in circular rows of seats, rising tier upon tier, and falling back in ascension like the walls of a wooden bowl. The dominant impression was the room's structure and the wooden-eye emptiness of the seats, the Jury taking a mere four rows of six seats each, besides which there were only present the Judge, Court Clerk, one or two minor attendants and a smattering of spectators, since these Hearings were, by and large, closed sessions. Above the top row of seats was a rim of sky-lights under the flat ceiling and, through the use of murals in concentrically graduated perspective, this had nearly the illusion of being vaulted.

The room was in silence when the Doctor entered with the attendant, the process having apparently reached a stage where nothing more could be done without the presence of the principal party. The two went directly to the wooden stand placed in the centre of the floor, just in front of the raised presidium where Judge Lester sat.

All thin and silver outside his black robes, Judge Lester would have borne a strong resemblance to the actor, Lewis Stone, except that he wore heavy, shell-rimmed glasses.

The attendant, addressing first the Judge, and then the Jury, which was seated in a body on the Judge's left, twenty-four variously dressed men and women, all seemingly serious and middle-aged, announced the Dr Eichner and indicated by a polite movement of his arm that he should take his place in the stand. The Doctor nodded gravely toward both Judge and Jury before stepping up into the low railed box.

'I am very sorry to be late,' he said. 'I was unexpectedly detained. I ask this Court's indulgence.' Here, he almost imperceptibly lowered his head, as in apology to the Court. This gesture, which was not without a certain old world dignity, was immediately followed by a whispery stirring in the Grand Jury box.

Judge Lester threw a look of caution toward that body and, softly clearing his throat, addressed Dr Eichner.

'The report of Police Officers Stockton and Fiske has been heard by this Jury—including your initial account of the accident—and finally, your statement before Captain Meyer as well. These are entered into Court Records and are, of course, available for your study. Naturally, it was desirable that you be present during this testimony, since whatever statement you may wish to make now could have perhaps been better arranged, more deliberately pertinent to the testimony already heard. However, [illegible] with relief that this mild-mannered man, and relatively young, was certainly not whom he had first wrongly supposed, a certain other Judge Lester, an obscure Justice who, several years ago, had come to notoriety through his severity in traffic violation cases, an undue severity, indeed, which had resulted at last in his impeachment.

'With your permission,' said Dr Eichner, confident even to bowing slightly toward the Judge who, in turn, acknowledged this by tilting one hand, fingers extended, up from the base of the palm, flashing the stark white of it against the black folds of his chest.

'As Judge Lester has suggested,' began Dr Eichner, speaking earnestly to the Jury who themselves at once settled back in attitudes of deliberate interest and comfort, 'it is to be regretted that I was not present to hear the testimony of Officers Stockton and Fiske. As for the reading of my statement before Chief Meyer, let me say first off, that, providing the proper *emphasis* and *intonation* were given that reading, the statement is adequate, and we need not elaborate on it today. Naturally, of course, I shall want to see Court Records account of both. And until then, I shall make no comment thereon which should be taken as *definitive*. Presumably, however, the testimony of Officers Stockton and Fiske here this morning would correspond to their report given to Chief Meyer — a report with which I am familiar — and which might be described as adequate *in fact* — so far as it goes — but, I'm afraid, entirely false in *spirit*. I say this without wishing to prejudice this Court, or any official who may be present, against these Officers. If their handling of this case was, in the strictest sense, improper, and deserves corrective attention — then let the departments concerned take note. It would be inopportune, however, for us to consider here the failure of these officers, in any other connection than as could serve to explain away the false emphasis drawn from certain circumstances surrounding this case — namely then, that their knowledge of these circumstances *was* . . . limited.

'Now, you are familiar with my statement before Chief Meyer. It is, substantially, correct. You have heard Judge Lester hesitate before the word, "accident." Advisedly so. I am prepared to maintain, indeed, to *insist*, upon the contrary: that here was no accident, but a deliberate attempt on my life, by persons unknown. One of these persons is now dead, in the city morgue, in a state beyond identification. Of the known parties to this conspiracy, however, this much may be said: one was a woman; two others, men — one of whom is perhaps also dead, or very seriously injured. My descriptions of each, as well as of the vehicle involved, are, of course, at the disposition of any authority concerned.'

The Doctor ended on a severe, almost reprimanding note; but, after a pause, he added with a smile of encouragement: 'We have a good deal to go on, you see, and these people, of course, will eventually be found.'

'Yes, yes,' said Judge Lester. 'The Jury may ask questions now.'

'Dr Richards,' the man blurted out, already half standing, but his attention was caught at once by the woman on his left who cupped her hands in a whisper.

'I mean, Dr Eig-ner,' continued the businessman and snickered embarrassedly. Some of the Jurors nearest him tittered, as in approval of the mistake, and Dr Eichner smiled condescendingly.

'Do you know of any reason why there should have been this attempt made on your life?' demanded the businessman, frowning heavily. 'I mean, do you know anyone who would have wanted to *kill you*?'

The rest of the Jury became respectfully attentive again, waiting, with the easy interest of young philosophy students.

'No,' said the Doctor earnestly, 'nor did I mean to imply as much. I did not, in fact, mean to imply that an attempt had been made on *my* life as such — though, of course, my opinion on this could not be properly brought out before your question. Let me now state, however, that to my knowledge I have no, shall we say, *mortal enemies*. The criminal aspect of this case is under investigation, of course; but, at this point, there occurs to me only one plausible explanation, the obvious one: *mistaken identity*.'

Perhaps it was merely a dramatic arrangement of the words, but many of the Jurors were visibly moved by the Doctor's statement, and whispered, as in his behalf, among themselves. Against this, however, a woman seated just in the middle of the body who had vied with the business-man for first question, and had kept her hand half raised during the Doctor's answer, now rose above the neigh-bouring looks of wonderment in a voice edged with accus-ation: 'Doctor, how fast would you estimate you were going at the point of the collision?'

'Let's clarify this question,' said Dr Eichner with spirited good nature. 'There were several "points-of-collision," though perhaps no more than three distinct ones, these occurring over the distance of a 16th mile or so. You have asked for an *estimate* of speed. Clearly, it will be only that—though I might add, that, as such, it will be rela-tively expert. Frankly, I anticipated this, if not as a ques-tion, then as a point of interest, and I have already made the calculations. I think I will ask your indulgence, how-ever, to mentally re-check these figures.'

And while the wrath on the woman's face appeared to soften towards annoyance, and around her some of the Jurors coughed and whispered, Judge Lester himself gently cleared his throat, and Dr Eichner was again in the attitude of concentrated thought, his head back, eyes half-closed, fingertips tremoring on the railing of the stand, but only for an instant. 'Yes, that is correct,' he said with finality. 'My estimates, then—for the speed at the points-of-collision: first point, 95; second, 112; and the third, 127.' Each figure was spoken distinctly and after a pause, evidently for the benefit of anyone taking notes; but was a whining woman-chorus of 'Why, I never!'

'What kind of car do you *drive*, Doctor?' asked the businessman in a voice that seemed too harsh for contempt alone.

'Delahaye 235,' said the Doctor, almost proudly; but his smile was modest, as though the two men had established a bond.

'*What* kind?' asked the chorus, turning cross on itself like a thin, wounded snake. And as the young man's voice was heard again to say 'souped-up!' Judge Lester spoke out mildly: 'Let us have order. The two cars involved, as stated in Officer's Report, were a Cadillac sedan, and a Delahaye. The Delahaye is a French sports car.'

When Judge Lester stopped speaking, the attention of the Jury seemed to remain with him as if he should have more to say on the matter. Several actually strained towards him in speechless anticipation, and then seemed to take his silence as an unleashing, for they all tried to speak at once, but almost as quickly gave way to the woman who had asked the important question, and who was still standing.

'Doctor, how did you happen to be going so fast in the *first* place?'

Dr Eichner's face clouded slightly. 'Fast?' There was

some confusion in his tone, which only then seemed overcome by friendly reproach. 'Perhaps our standards are different,' he said quietly. 'By "first *place*," however, I assume you mean the first point of collision? The speed there we've estimated at 95 . . .' Here his voice trailed away and, though not at a loss, he gave a shrug, merely as if there were nothing more to add.

'And don't you consider that just *a-little-fast*, Doctor?' The businessman spoke out so sharply that for one electric moment everything seemed to hinge on the Doctor's response.

Yet he did not falter, but only gazed at the man with curious interest before replying: 'In what sense? Certainly not in the *legal* sense—our concern here—since there is no lawful requirement, or limitation, of speed on the Canyon Drive between Wilshire and Drexal. That is correct, is it not, Judge Lester?'

'Yes, that is true,' said the Judge, who was leaning forward now in close attention, and he continued after a pause:. 'I do not consider the question, however, necessarily improper.'

'*I* do not consider the question necessarily improper,' Dr Eichner agreed, speaking with restrained enthusiasm to Judge Lester, as though the two of them were comfortably before an open fire, alone, about to savour some Old Port and metaphysics. 'It is a *personal* question, however, and I think our best approach to it is a semantic one. I would have to ask the Juror what he intends by his word, *fast*?' And so, returning to the questioner with a tolerant smile, the Doctor continued. '*Fast*, you mean, no doubt, as opposed to *slow*. But I would have to ask you: which said the Doctor affably. 'Still, we mustn't anticipate the relative-value, must we? And yet I *will* anticipate, that by automobile, you mean *my* automobile or *an* automobile of its type: straight-six with an FIA Class D displacement. In which case, the answer is: No, it is not fast. A glance at last year's record sheets for the Le Mans and Biarritz runs will reassure you on that point; or again, at the Official Log of flat-trials at Salt Lake, available, I believe, in our Public Library.'

When the Doctor ended, the Jury seemed embarrassedly quiet, immobile, some staring at the Doctor with that open, hopelessly committed wonder which ragged children hold for people eating cake, while the eyes of the others turned beseechingly to the presidium, from where Judge Lester, his head slightly to the side, a faint smile on his lips, asked in a curious voice: 'How *did* you happen to be going at that speed, Doctor? In the first place,' he added, a bit colloquially, so that there was at least a sheen of innocent levity over the question, and from somewhere in the Jury then, came one, isolated laugh, raucous, but buried and irrelevant, as the rest of the body seemed to relax into confidence again.

'In point of fact,' the Doctor took him up, certainly with a trace of outward malice, 'since it has been recorded—by our estimate, granted—that the initial speed, that is, the speed of the "first place," was 95, while the others were: 112 and 127 respectively, I think we may safely say that it was not *fast*, but, indeed, *relatively* slow.'

This drew a strange laugh from a part of the Jury, a blind and desperate laugh, as though now they were laughing at the possible ridicule of Judge Lester, who himself smiled, a little painfully. But all this suddenly changed when the one apparently Negro member of the Jury, a properly dressed man, who had followed the proceedings with straightfaced attentiveness, leaned toward his neighbour and said aloud: 'Ah cain' heah! Do he say: *slow*? Or do he say: *flyin' low*?'

Here was a recognisable attempt to be a party to things, and about half the Jury laughed uproariously.

'How's that?' asked Dr Eichner, not having correctly heard, but wanting, with a searching smile, to be in on the joke too. And the Jury laughed again, this time with a kind of savagery.

A part of the Jury, however, did *not* laugh but, like the Negro, maintained very straight-faces, as if they were consciously refusing to laugh at what was ordinarily laughable; and Dr Eichner may have taken this combination of laughter and the show of plain serious faces as interest and allegiance, for he proceeded in the next few sentences dangerously to incriminate himself.

'The speed, then, was 95. As a matter of personal curiosity, however, I don't mind telling you the circumstances of that particular figure.' He paused, and then began anew, speaking with brisk confidence. 'I know this stretch of drive,' he said firmly. 'I time my descent, from one-eighth mile, on the light at Drexal, a five-second duration. This calls for an average of 97.5. Now then. I pass, which, as I stated in my earlier account, it failed, or refused, to do. Then, of course, when I made my bid . . .'

'I'm sorry,' interrupted Judge Lester with a look of discomfort on his face. 'You say you *timed* your descent against the light, Doctor. What do you mean by that, exactly?'

'Correct me if I'm wrong,' replied the Doctor. 'I don't believe I said "*against* the light," but rather "*on* the light." or perhaps, "*by* the light".'

'But you were, in fact, racing the light? Isn't that so?'

'No. No, I could not express it that way. You imply an element of competition which, in fact, was not present. The light was, as it *is*, of course, a fixture, a mechanical implement. I was *using* that fixture to *time my descent*; exactly, I believe, as I stated.'

Judge Lester had started forward, as in exasperation, a finger raised to press the question, when the Jury suddenly exploded in a disorder of mixed comment:

'He was trying to beat the light when it happened!'

'Where does he think this is?'

'Running a red light!'

'*He's* not so dumb!'

'Ran the light.'

'Yeah, *he's* crazy—like a fox!'

'Not as dumb as he makes out!'

Judge Lester rapped for order with his gavel, at the same time shuffling some papers before him.

'If I'm not mistaken,' he said evenly, 'this is an aspect of the incident which you failed to bring out in your earlier statements, both to the Officers and to Captain Meyer. Is that not correct?'

'I can't go along with that phrasing,' said Dr Eichner, irritably. ' "*Failed*?" No, I withheld the fact, if you like. And advisedly so. To have done otherwise would have served no constructive end in point of law, while, psychologically, it would simply have pointed up the already misplaced emphasis which the Officers had given the circumstances. I've had a decent amount of training in fundamental psychology, you see, and I-think-I-know-when ...'

'That's sophistry,' said the loud young whisper that had earlier said 'souped-up.' And, as suddenly, a man who looked like a farmer, in the centre of the body, lurched himself forward, speaking abruptly, his face a scrubbed red leather. 'What I want to know, and what I believe the *rest* of this Jury wants to know, without all this two-faced double talk, is whether or not you were trying to BEAT THAT LIGHT!'

Dr Eichner sighed aloud. It was evident he had begun to tire. 'No,' he said wearily. 'No, decidedly not. You apparently imagine the traffic-light to be something other than a useful mechanism. Perhaps you see it as a *living* thing, whose intelligence and attitude somehow represent a threat ... to me, and with whom my relationship necessarily is one of combat. Now, is this my attitude? Or is it your attitude? Or, indeed, is it not simply the attitude admissable, for "trying" implies *risk* or possible failure as a point of my attitude. This is not within your prerogative. You may say, if you like, simply that I *was* "beating the light." The choice of words is, of course, your own affair.'

'Boy, is that sophistry!' said the young man. 'Dig that sophistry!'

'Oh yeah?' challenged another blindly, 'like a *fox*!'

'In any event, it is not a point of law,' the Doctor continued. 'Our attitudes are quite outside the law.'

'It's against the law to deliberately race against a red-light, I can tell you that!' said a young woman in a smart print.

'No,' replied the Doctor sympathetically enough, 'let me reassure you on that head; it is not. Regardless of how we may agree or disagree as to the wording, one thing is certain: on an un-zoned stretch of road, you could not have a *race*—you see the contradiction we come up against.'

'You'd see the one you'd be up against if a tyre blew out at that speed and you ran over and killed a little boy or girl on his way home from school! I think he ought to be locked up!'

'Fournier blues,' said the Doctor firmly, 'do not blow out. This is a matter of record. Moreover, school-children

seldom cross un-zoned drives haphazardly. I'm afraid you do their training an injustice.'

'And suppose he was simply walking along the side of the road? On his way home from school? How would *you* feel?' The woman was visibly near tears.

'Madame,' said the Doctor softly, 'with all due respect for your feelings on the matter, I must ask Judge Lester to remind you that this is a *court of law.* As a point of information, however, it so happens that the nearest *school* to Drexal and Canyon Drive is Westwood Catholic, five miles distant, and it is, correct me if I am wrong, a boarding school.'

'It is evident,' said Judge Lester, raising his mild voice to intervene, 'that this Hearing could be protracted, *ad infinitum* so to speak. And it *may* be that a reconvening will be in order. For the moment, however, I am prepared to suggest that the Jury retire and consider the findings.' The Judge stopped and sorted his papers again. 'I would like to put one last question to the principal party,' he continued then, looking directly at the Doctor. 'Doctor, you said that you "know this stretch of road." I assume then it is a customary route with you. Is it a daily route?'

'It is *daily*,' replied the Doctor, 'five days a week. It is usually twice daily, both ways; that is to say, I most often take lunch at home.'

'I see. Now. Is it your habit—and by habit, I mean simply the frequency of occurrence—to time your descent on the light at Drexal?'

'On the eastward, or return route, yes. On the west route, no. The west route does not, strictly speaking, *descend* on Drexel, but is an almost level approach, with

The issues here are not too well defined, but deliberation at this point may be fruitful in that respect. In any event, we will want to have some lunch now. Will the foreman-designate lead the Jury through this door, please.' The Judge ended, gesturing toward a small door between himself and the Jury, whereupon the businessman on the lower left rose and, with a formal bow in the direction of both the Judge and the Doctor, turned stiffly and began the procession through the small brown door.

'Doctor,' said Judge Lester raising his voice matter-of-factly above the scuffling, 'you may wish to have some lunch, in the cafeteria on the second floor : through the door you entered and up the stairs on your right. You will please return to the anteroom before two o'clock.'

Then the two men exchanged little nods, rather curt, and each stepped off his stand and went in different directions, the Judge through a small brown door, identical, though opposite, to the one through which the Jury was passing; while the Doctor himself went back out through the big front door he had come in by.

CHAPTER IX

BACK at the Clinic, just at the moment the Grand Jury was retiring, Babs Mintner was in Nurses Rest Rooms changing from her white habit into street clothes, preparing to take leave, this being Saturday noon.

Near the corner sofa farthest from the window stood a lacquered straw screen, provided for this very purpose: of these young women nurses changing in and out of their habits. This was suitable since all of them — with the exception of the nurses-in-residence, Eleanor Thorne and Beth Jackson — lived out. Now, however, Babs Mintner could only take half advantage of the screen in standing to one side of it, talking with Nurse Thorne who sat bright and clear-eyed, but rather stern, on the sofa close by.

'That's a charming blouse,' said Nurse Thorne, as the girl drew a light grey shirt-waist over her head. 'Where did you find it?' And her look narrowed to scrutiny.

'It *wasn't* exactly what I wanted,' Babs began, shaking her curls defensively, but smiling as she stepped easily in front of the mirror, tucking the edges into her dark blue skirt.

'Oh, it's lovely,' insisted Nurse Thorne in genuine admiration.

'But I do like it,' Babs continued matter-of-factly, turning this way and that before the glass, touching her hair and tossing it once, perhaps to free it from any interference it might have received in putting on the blouse.

was changing.

'I hope I'm not speaking out of turn, Barbara,' Eleanor said, pressing the first snap firmly closed, '. . . that is, I'm sure you won't take offence, but . . . well, you can understand my position here, I mean, the responsibility, my responsibility to the staff. . . ' Her eyes searched the glass, where Bab's face was now a mask of blushing innocence, and went on at once in a lighter tone: 'Beth — Nurse Jackson — was suggesting that there might be some reason to feel that, well, that one of our young men was *bothering* you.' She finished hurriedly, working with the snaps, but immediately raised her eyes again to the glass to fasten them hard and metal-bright in the soft, wide blueness of the girl's own. And Babs gave a start of indignation:

'*Me?* Well, *I never*. . . *Beth* said that? *I* was bothered? But what did she *say*?'

'Oh, I assured her she was exaggerating,' Nurse Thorne hastened, soothing the girl, a hand on her shoulder, 'that if there *had* been some indiscretion — well, you would have come to me.'

Barbara simply flushed crimson at this and lowered her great eyes.

'— that if *he* should,' continued Nurse Thorne, 'and I won't call any names here, or if *any of them* should . . .

say anything improper to you, or make — *advances.* Well! You ought to tell me about it immediately!'

At this, Babs seemed to recover entirely, or at least enough to look again into the glass, pleasant and surprised.

'I'm referring, of course,' continued Nurse Thorne, a bit irritably, 'to that boy in the Pharmacy, Mr Edward's nephew. *Ralph.*' Whereupon Babs resumed her toilet, brushing her hair now, smiling carelessly, and even managing an airy laugh of protest. 'No!' she cried gaily, 'not *that* — excuse me — not him! Good heavens, how *could* Beth! Oh, really, it's too funny!' And she brushed her hair merrily. 'Really!' She turned brightly to face Nurse Thorne, who regarded the girl now with a disturbed smile.

'Naturally,' said the elder woman, 'I wasn't suggesting that *you* were interested in *him.* What I was getting at is: has *he* made any sort of overtures . . . to *you?*'

'Him?' cried Babs, crossing the room for her purse. 'Why, how on earth could he? Oh, I mean, I suppose so! You know how boys are . . . Why, I wouldn't have noticed it!' she declared finally, as though she had hit upon it; and in the moment of her triumph, she turned again, ingenuous, to face Eleanor Thorne, and looking every inch the American dream-girl, trim almost to masculine in the tapered blue gaberdine skirt, and in the weblike pearl of her shirt-waist inviolate.

'Then there *was* something,' said Eleanor, looking away now, keeping her voice casual, though her face was terribly dark the while.

'But, Eleanor,' Babs pleaded, tossing her pretty head

longer frowning, touched her shoulder, while Babs' eyes remained so wide with the wonder of it all.

'You look lovely,' said Eleanor, the edge of her voice a tremor. 'It's a wonderful effect,' speaking then as she gently touched the blouse-front, a net of sheen grey fainter than pearl, a dove-down diaphanous grey, fashioned, as it were, to hold in a web of insinuation that treasure nest of lace, the wide-bordered blue nylon slip which itself showed budding through the sheen as a filigree, an impossible perfection of softness, and a promise.

'I do like it,' admitted Babs, as though she were being quite frankly objective, looking toward the mirror, touching her hair. She stepped away from Nurse Thorne then to the mirror, and leaned peering into it as if she might have caught something amiss from the distance; but, at the glass it proved to be nothing, a fleck, or a shadow, and she sighed good-naturedly, and shrugged, perhaps slightly exasperated at her own flawlessness. Then, snapping the purse shut, she started for her coat in a surge of high spirits.

'Good heavens, I've got to run!' she cried, looking at her watch with feigned alarm. 'That poor man won't know whether he's coming or going! I *am* awful!' And she beamed her mischievous-child best at Eleanor Thorne, but the other was still disturbed. 'Barbara,' she said evenly, 'a girl as attractive as you are should be very careful, where men are concerned, *very* careful.'

'I'll say!' said Babs, knowingly grave at the door, caught up for one moment in the other's seriousness; but as quickly became quite gay. 'Here today, gone tomorrow!' she cried airily. 'And good riddance to bad rubbish; they're such babies, really.'

'Be sweet, dear,' said Nurse Thorne with a trace of grim sadness, and she leaned over to kiss the girl on the cheek, being careful not to muss her, but squeezing her shoulder quite hard.

'Bye now!' said Babs, smiling wholeheartedly and raising her hand, as she pushed open the door and was gone.

Nurse Thorne crossed the room to the sofa, and lay down there, one hand covering her half-closed, glittering eyes.

CHAPTER X

BY THE time Babs reached the Clinic veranda and started down the front steps, it was evident that her excitement had lessened; her appearance no longer expressed the bubbling-over-with-the-sheer-joy-of-living which so marked her presence among others. Walking alongside the wide pebble drive now she seemed, less determinedly, a real part of things, her light coat neatly over her arm, the flat purse clasped firmly against her little rib-case, and was, after all, never quite alone. And justly so perhaps, for as she approached the gate-walk now, her shoulders tremored and straightened slightly in the animal-like awareness of another presence, and, as a car drew near, overtaking her on the drive behind, along the back curve of her legs she seemed to feel each stocking-seam glisten and lie taut and ready as a stringed arrow.

It was Ralph Edwards, in his room-mate's convertible.

'Hello there,' he said, slowing alongside Babs, then stopping the car a few yards ahead. He pushed the door open towards her. 'Come on, I'll give you a lift.' He had spoken quite casually, with no trace of his usual grin.

The girl's next step was in the direction of the car-door, but she stopped, as though it had been involuntary, and asked, almost irritably : 'Why, which way are you going?'

'Well, I meant to the bus-stop,' said Ralph, frowning. '. . . I'm going over to the school, but if there's someplace I can drop you . . .' He glanced at his watch, '. . . I probably have time . . .'

'Oh, you needn't bother about that,' said Babs, looking into the distance. 'It's such a lovely day!' she smiled radiantly at the things around, and for a moment, seemed on the verge of hugging herself; then, she let her smile complete the circle and come to rest on the young man's face, as if he too must share in this good fortune of life.

'Well, come on,' he said, leaning toward the open door again clearly impatient. 'I can drop you somewhere.'

She laughed, as though the court-idiot had thrown some odd-penny pearls at her feet. 'No, really,' she touched at her hair, looking vaguely beyond him again. 'It's such a lovely day . . .'

'Please, Barbara,' said the boy earnestly, 'I want to *talk* to you.'

Babs looked at him searchingly, perhaps as she would at a small boy whose antics were somewhat amusing, but not understandable. On the seat beside Ralph Edwards, like a lowered arm-rest that would be between them, was a large book. Then, without seeming to acknowledge the heart-felt desperation his tone belied, she got onto the seat, though quite close to the door of her own side. 'Well, I wouldn't mind for a little,' she said, still beaming. 'It's such a nice day for a drive.' And they were off.

At the wheel, Ralph Edwards, as though responding to the surge of power beneath his feet and hands, put away his show of humility almost at once. 'I had to come get a book,' he said, explaining. 'I left it at the Dispensary yesterday,' and, proving it, he nodded, with a rather heavy nonchalance toward the great mouse-grey text-book that lay on the seat between them, then picked it up and put it on the floor under the seat. 'An exam this afternoon,' he went on, 'in Bio-chem.'

As they turned out into the Boulevard, picking up speed, the wind settled in wide sweeping drafts over the front glass of the convertible and broke fiercely across their faces through the lowered side-windows. It was apparent that Babs' hair was going to suffer terribly, and [illegible] more sense,' she said firmly, then settled down to look fixedly out that side of the car.

For a moment Ralph concentrated on his driving; then after glancing once or twice at Babs, he began to hum, being blasé, drumming his finger-tips over the top of the steering-wheel. He switched on the radio, found a popular dance-tune programme, 'The Make-Believe Ballroom,' and raised his humming in confidence. 'Like dancing?' he asked the girl, careful not to take his eyes off the road.

'Me?' answered Babs with a laugh that was at once careless and surprised. 'Love it!' she said authoritatively, and she began to hum along with the music herself, looking straight ahead.

Ralph Edwards turned his eyes full on her, taking it all in entirely. He started to speak, but when his voice caught he laughed embarrassedly and reached at his shirt-pocket for a cigarette.

'Smoke?' he asked, proffering the pack, but in having kept his eyes on the girl for too long, and now in proffering the cigarettes, he allowed the car to drift onto the shoulder of the road, and had to swerve it awkwardly to avoid the mound of a stone-marker.

Meanwhile, Babs, pretending not to notice, replied over all the noise and bumping. 'I don't smoke, thank you.'

'You don't smoke?' asked Ralph, trying to salvage that advantage, as though nothing had happened. 'Really?' He forced a tired smile, to suggest that she was perhaps too virtuous for him; Babs, however, was still so absorbed in not noticing, that she failed to catch even his words.

'*And,* you don't talk much either, do you?' the boy hurried on, pursuing it. 'Now why is that?' He gave her his tooth-paste smile, but Babs continued to hum, not looking his way at all.

They stopped for a light then, at a quiet intersection where the signal seemed interminably red.

'Say, do you know this guy Eichner?' Ralph asked suddenly in his schoolboy voice. With the motor idling, he sounded much louder than before.

Babs gave a start and looked anxiously about outside. 'Who, *Fred?* Why, how do you mean?'

On the corner nearest the car, where a boy was knelt to one knee in untying a bundle of afternoon papers, the cloth bag, colour of orange sherbet with worn black markings lay furled in the sun at his feet.

Ralph laughed, a bit jerkily. '*Fred?* Sure, old Doc Fred Eichner! Sure, they've got him down before the Grand Jury. My uncle was telling me about it. He was in a big car-wreck the other day.'

Babs was sitting up straight, toward the edge of her seat. '*Today?* Oh, why didn't they tell me?' she demanded, and continued practically unheard. 'Fred. Oh, I've got to be . . . Where is it?' she implored then of the boy.

'Well, at the Court House, I suppose,' Ralph answered,

[illegible] cried Babs, and for the first time really embraced him in an ecstatic smile.

'Sure,' said Ralph Edwards, warming toward the idea, and as the light went green, he started the car with a forward surge that gently lifted the girl's feet and knees, but only for an instant.

CHAPTER XI

WHEN the old man in the Information booth told Babs and Ralph that Dr Eichner's hearing 'wasn't over with yet,' Babs evinced a theatrically mixed reaction of sharp relief and dramatic, almost maternal resolve.

'Well, what are we waiting for?' she demanded of Ralph, as though his faltering now were despicable, and she led their way in a march down the corridor beyond the glass door.

They reached 8th Sessions antechamber at that propitious moment of recess between the departure of the sweepers and the arrival of the minor officials, and so were able to enter the empty courtroom almost unnoticed.

In the centre of the room, standing by the box that had held Dr Eichner, Babs looked anxiously about, apparently expecting the drama to unfold abruptly now at any moment.

'Guess the Jury's still out deliberating,' said Ralph gravely, but the great emptiness of the room seemed to gradually and so completely absorb the girl's authority and initiative that now she stood before him as if she hadn't heard. Then Ralph indicated the nearest seats for them and even half turned the girl in that direction she seemed so utterly helpless.

'Oh, if we could only *do* something,' she pleaded.

Ralph looked at her curiously. 'Don't worry,' he said, his voice soft; and then, with a real tenderness, he put a hand on her shoulder, saying : 'It will be all right,' whereupon she raised her eyes to his in comfort, as if he were then the one person in the world who understood. And he took her hand in his own.

No sooner was Babs graciously seated than all the court personages, with a seeming sort of regal demien not attendant upon the earlier session — perhaps because they had all now just comfortably eaten — began their serious entrance : the striding minor officials, holding their girth in strict correctness; the court reporters, looking less sleepy than before, and less cynical, perhaps even hoping now to construe something of the day worth while; the great newly-confident Jury, and the few privileged spectators, both parties having struck up fresh acquaintances during lunch and bringing to the case at hand a novel enthusiasm, as if to mirror their own lonely importance; and, finally, the constant Judge Lester, magnificent in his black, and Doctor Frederick Eichner, both remarkable men to look upon.

obviously took no notice. He resumed his place by the side of the stand and waited for Judge Lester, mounting the high presidium, to be seated.

The Jury was still in a mood of recess, with whisperings and coughings among them, while Judge Lester shifted the papers about before him.

On the far side of the Jury box, a spectator was standing in conversation with one of the Jurors. They were both young men, talking lightly, with many smiles and gestures between them. The Doctor had mounted the stand and was looking interestedly around, in his expression no hint of anxiety, when suddenly he started forward clutching the rail, and in an instant, his face seemed suddenly to go ashen with bitter incredulity.

'If you *please!*' he said in a harsh voice to Judge Lester and, facing the Jury box, he pointed a severely accusing hand at the young man who was speaking to the Juror. And it was none other than Felix Treevly.

For the moment, the Doctor seemed beside himself with speechless contempt, and, as though his accusing hand were itself enough to confiscate the man, kept it stiffly extended, quaking in mute condemnation of Mr Treevly. 'What, in God's name, is that man doing here?' he demanded then, managing to assert some control over himself. 'This is a closed session, is it not? Your Honour,

I am forced to challenge the *integrity* of this Jury!'

This outbreak caused great consternation in the court-room. Almost everyone in the Jury sat agog, and the young Juror to whom Mr Treevly had been talking, glared with open hostility at the Doctor, whereas Treevly himself, in acknowledging Dr Eichner's remarks, merely smiled with strained politeness and nodded. 'The Doctor isn't telling all he *knows*,' he said then in a very quiet voice, his lips formed by the pained smile which did not leave them throughout the incident. And, so saying, he turned his face slightly to profile, striking an odd pose, but also showing a glimpse of the small white patch on the back of his head.

'Yes, I know!' countered the Doctor at once. 'I know that abrasion! What have you packed it with? Spider-eggs? Good Lord!' He leaned heavily pale against the railing, as if he were going to be sick.

'You *would* like to think so, wouldn't you, Doctor?' replied Treevly, only his mouth carrying the fantastic smile, for his dull eyes were a flat dead grey. 'Or *would* it upset you? Would it upset you — and your *very-special-knowledge?*'

Judge Lester raised his gavel, but before he could strike, Mr Treevly softly repeated the phrase: 'The Doctor isn't telling all he *knows*,' whereupon Dr Eichner, recovering, spoke out so plainly that Judge Lester held the gavel, suspended as it were, above the Doctor's words.

'I *will* tell this much,' he shouted, 'this man is a serious mental case: a vicious *pederast*, in a state of advanced paranoia!'

'That's slanderous!' cried Treevly's friend in the Jury

'I advise *you,* Doctor,' said Judge Lester in a very loud voice, 'that you may be liable to contempt of this Court!' And he struck deafeningly with his gavel. 'I'm going to insist upon order here!' And as the courtroom grew quiet again, only Dr Eichner's voice was heard speaking to one of the officials sitting near. 'Detain that man. I want to question him.' He spoke in such confident undertones, however, that it is doubtful if the official, one of the record clerks, even heard him. In any event, he confronted the Doctor with an ice-cold silence. Judge Lester had heard, however, and was quick to react. 'I said, *order,* Doctor; I'll not warn you again!' He fixed Dr Eichner in a hard, formulative gaze which remained unbroken for fully half a minute. The Doctor however, no longer seemed to be with them. His aggressive presence had given over to an obviously deep preoccupation; his eyes stared into the Jury without focus, brow furrowed, wholly reflective, as if in his mind's-eye now he would thread the loosened strands of an intricate pattern.

'It is conceivable,' Judge Lester began, after clearing his throat, 'that, had developments here taken another course, your *challenge* of the Jury might be well taken . . . these are closed-sessions, and I *will* have something to say to the Guards responsible for the admission of unauthorized persons . . . However, it has been decided that the issues and the evidence in this case are, at the present time, too vague and too incomplete to indicate a definite finding. Therefore, a second hearing will be in order. I am going to set this hearing for ten days from today, that is Monday, May 2nd, by which time, it is probable, the District Attorney's Office will have carried their investigations to a more conclusive point — so that the issues and evidence will be a great deal more clear.

'The present Jury will not be called again. The principal party will receive summons on the day previous to the Hearing.' Judge Lester paused and looked at the Jury before speaking seriously to them. 'Jury service is the duty and privilege of every good citizen. Our democratic tenets greatly depend upon honouring this duty, safeguarding this privilege. On behalf of the government and people of the County of Los Angeles, I would like to express gratitude then to those of you here today for your sacrifice and co-operation.

'The Court is dismissed.'

'What does it mean?' Babs whispered to Ralph squeezing his hand as though accidently, and looking helpless again, when they rose with the others. He squeezed her hand in return, to show understanding, and they both looked around for Dr Eichner. But the Doctor had already swept past them and, as they saw now, was disappearing out the door, trying to overtake someone ahead. Apparently it was Felix Treevly he was after.

ing, no longer holding hands, Ralph took the girl's arm, pressing it gently, whereupon she edged away, raising her eyes with the quick look of a small friend betrayed.

'What's the matter?' asked Ralph, letting his annoyance show. He should have been in the library, of course, studying for his examination.

When Babs didn't answer, but instead allowed her preoccupation with bigger things be suggested, the boy at once became sulky and morose; so, at the bottom of the steps, Babs suddenly touched his sleeve, to detain him, while she looked anxiously around, as though she expected someone to be waiting.

'Listen. What is this Eichner to you, anyway?' asked Ralph, putting his hands on his hips. 'A particular friend or something?'

Babs gave a start. 'Who, *Fred?*' And she turned her blue eyes up on him like saucers of hope and confusion. 'Why, no! Why?' She said it in such a way that he could not possibly have believed her — though, actually, it was true — and she gave him a long, inquiring look, shifting it from one part of his face to another, as if searching for a meaning beneath the words.

Ralph had seemed ready to say goodbye and turn on his heel. Now that she was looking at him though, he stood firm, and responded with an appreciative gaze of his own. Babs had raised one finger to her cheek and held it there in an attitude of studied curiosity.

'I don't know,' said Ralph finally, looking hurt again and half turning away, 'you seemed pretty interested.'

'Silly!' she cried, touching his arm and moving her head back with a little laugh.

'Well, let's have a drink,' said Ralph, at a complete loss now, and too, as if looking at her made him thirsty.

'*Coffee* for me, thank you very much!' Babs said archly, and followed it with a knowing smile.

So they began to walk again, though this time, for the moment at least, Ralph carefully avoided touching her, even when they crossed the street. But at the opposite side, he put his hand on her elbow as they stepped up the curb.

'*Thank* you,' said Babs and gave him a mischievous smile, to show she knew perfectly well what he was up to.

CHAPTER XIII

BACK at the Clinic, behind the closed door of his consultation room, Dr Eichner was having a talk with Martin Frost, private detective.

'I'm badly mistaken if there's a connection between them,' Fred Eichner was saying, 'but one thing is certain — however, let me persist in offering you a drink.'

Martin Frost raised a hand. 'Not when I'm on the job, thanks, never touch it. You say he's a *pervert?*'

his late forties, apparently not given to facial expressions of any sort — a trait which may have accounted for the flaccid spread of his great face being, as it was, without a single line or wrinkle. 'I see your point,' he said, merely lowering his eyes toward the floor to show the seriousness he felt for the case.

'I want you to get a line on this man,' Dr Eichner continued grandly. 'Get-a-line-on-him. We'll need to determine the exact nature of his association with that Juror, and so on. Naturally, you'll want to document any evidence of perversion that may come up. If a slander case is brought, at least we'll be ready on *that* head!'

The prospect seemed to warm the Doctor all over, and he snuggled comfortably in his chair, gently rolling the crystal glass between four extended fingers.

'By the way, what is your fee, Mr Frost?'

'I can give you a day-rate if you like, Doctor,' said Martin Frost, clearing his throat and trading the balance of his strapping bulk from one hip to another, 'of thirty-five and expenses . . . I'm not handling any other cases right now, so I could give it the full day, which is the way I like to work actually — one case at a time.'

'Good!'

'Keep things straight that way,' Martin Frost looked at his powerful hands. '. . . and concentrate.'

'Just so! Yes. Tell me, what was your last case, Mr Frost? If you're at liberty to say, of course.'

'As a matter of fact, I'm not. Most of my cases are entirely confidential, you see. I don't mind telling you, though, that I worked on the Beaton-Beaton case — you may have read about it in the papers not long ago.'

'Oh yes. Yes, of course. I was *wondering* who broke that case.'

'Well, naturally, I wasn't alone in it. The police, I mean. Yes, there were a lot of spoons in the fire on that one all right!'

Dr Eichner sipped from the glass with contemplative ease before he spoke again.

'Thirty-five a day? And expenses. Now, just what . . .'

Martin Frost sat forward, a white giant, clearing his throat. 'By expenses, Doctor, we mean any expense we would not ordinarily, or otherwise, incur — taxi-fares, tips, camera work, tapes, small bribes — which are sometimes necessary — and so forth, depending on the nature of the case, naturally. In this instance, I foresee no undue expense — though, of course, you would get an itemized account of these — and, naturally, we try to keep them at a minimum.'

'We have ten days to break this case,' said Dr Eichner emphatically, as though he weren't listening. 'That is the interval, you see, between today's hearing and the next convening of the Jury.'

'Well, Doctor,' Martin Frost began, looking down once more to his hands, which turned slowly above his lap like two heavy, spitted things, 'I see no reason why it can't be done.'

finger across his foremost right-hand knuckle, which cracked then like the split of a great hollow nut.

CHAPTER XIV

BABS and Ralph got back into the convertible and drove two blocks to a big fashionable Drive-In, where Ralph, with his right arm stretched along the back of the seat above Babs shoulders, ordered beer, and Babs, as she had threatened she might, a cup of coffee.

'Do you like Boston Coffee?' she asked the young man brightly.

'You mean coffee with a lot of cream?'

'Half cream, half coffee,' she informed him.

'Yes, I guess so. Do you?'

'Love it!' She spoke with worldly defiance, as though they had been talking about hashish or heroin.

'You could have had some now,' observed Ralph, too dryly.

'Why, how do you mean?'

'Well,' he explained, 'you could have ordered that instead of plain coffee.'

'Oh, not in the mood,' said Babs. 'I forgot to tell you,' she confided smartly, 'I'm moody!' And she beamed at him, her blue eyes all wet sparkles of starry promise.

'Listen, Babs,' he suddenly began, a plaintive softness to his voice, while her own look turned to wide-eyed surprise, as if a girl never knew what to expect, and as he was about to let his arm down to touch her shoulder, the waitress appeared with their tray, and they both seemed to withdraw slightly with little sighs of relief.

'I'll have half of it and then make it Boston,' Babs announced a minute later as she gazed up over her cup at the boy. Ralph smiled awkwardly but said nothing, drinking his beer in well spaced gulps, glancing at his wristwatch once or twice. When he passed the cream to Babs, she let their fingers touch lingeringly, though without seeming to notice it herself, all the while maintaining a spritely commentary on things at hand. It was as though she had religiously drawn her idea of conversation from the radio commercials, and now feared anathema if dead-air were allowed. 'You're a funny boy,' she said, not unkindly.

'How do you mean?' asked Ralph, trying to show some surprise.

'Well, I don't know,' said Babs, looking serious to gain time, 'you're so — quiet.' Then she laughed animatedly, touching his arm to reassure him. 'Not that there's anything wrong with that! I mean, good night, the way *I* rattle on so it isn't funny! And here *I* should be listening to *you*!'

'Well —' Ralph began uneasily.

'Eleanor Thorne — you know Eleanor, don't you?

'She's the Head Nurse, isn't she?'

'Yes, and she's really a wonderful person. So many of the girls don't like her — they say she's a holy-terror — but, oh, she's just absolu — '

Ralph had lowered his arm stealthily, and he leaned forward now in a half-hearted attempt to kiss the girl, exerting some pressure to bring her towards him. But Babs pulled away quickly, flushing and looking cross. '*Oh, no,*' she said, glancing furtively around at the other cars to see if she were being observed, then turning to look at Ralph as one bewildered and forlorn. 'I'm afraid I'm not the kind of a girl you think,' she said and waited.

'I only wanted to kiss you, Babs. You're so — *so* beautiful,' he explained miserably.

'Really!' said Babs, turning away to stare out the window like a sullen princess, actually quite pleased.

'But it's only natural, isn't it, Babs? I mean, what's wrong with it?'

'Well, I like *that!*' she said, looking at him again. 'I mean, it isn't as though we're on a *date*, is it?'

'Well, let's *have* a date,' suggested Ralph. 'Tonight.'

'What, so you can kiss me? Hmph! No thanks! Thanks a lot, but no than —'

'No, I wouldn't kiss you if you didn't want to,' promised

Ralph. 'It's just that I'd like to be *with* you and, well—I mean, we could have a lot of *fun* together.'

'Tonight!' said Babs. 'Honestly! Isn't that pretty short notice?'

'Not when two people like each other, Babs,' said Ralph, sounding wretched.

'Yes, I suppose that's how you do with your blonde girl friend, call her up the same day you want a date!' She eyed him keenly, then turned to stare out the window again. 'Well, not everyone is like that, thank you,' she said and seemed about to cry.

Ralph squeezed her shoulder gently. 'Babs, please,' he begged. 'I want to be with you so much—but listen, I have to go back to school now, for an exam, and, well, couldn't I pick you up later and we could go somewhere?'

'Honestly,' exclaimed Babs, 'I think it's simply terrible, asking girls to break dates. How would you feel if I broke a date on you?'

'Oh, you already have a date then?'

'Well, really!' said Babs, truly insulted at last.

Ralph paid, and they silently drove away, after Babs, in seeming reluctance, had given him her address. A few minutes later she began to make bright conversation again, which Ralph interrupted, saying sullenly: 'You just don't like me.'

'I *do* like you,' said Babs matter-of-factly, and then, with resentment, 'but you'd think I was terrible, giving you a date on such short notice. I know how boys think!'

'But I wouldn't!' said Ralph, 'I wouldn't!'

'Hmph!' said Babs.

still we were together, and it was nice. Do you see what I mean?'

'Yes, it was nice,' Babs admitted wistfully. 'I mean, it was so nice of you to do it. Oh, I *hope* everything is all right for Fred—Dr Eichner. Wasn't it terrible?'

'Please Babs,' Ralph pleaded, 'just this once, and from now on I'll ask you weeks ahead of time.'

'Well,' said Babs, sighing in surrender, 'I just hope you don't get any wrong ideas about it.'

Ralph beamed, and Babs continued, seriously emphasizing the understatement of it. 'I mean, it's *not* exactly something I'm in the habit of *doing*!'

CHAPTER XV

At 6.30, not more than four hours since their first meeting, Martin Frost was again talking to Dr Eichner, this time by phone. His voice sounded thick.

'I don't like it, Doc,' he admitted. 'I *don't* like the looks-of-it.'

'Where are you now, Frost?'

'Mayfair Room . . . Why don't you come on down?'

'I see. Good. Now, what's he doing — at this minute? You can see him, of course, from where you are?'

'*He's* at the bar, sipping his martini as pretty as you please — with his *friend*!' There was a bitter edge in Frost's thick mimicry, and an almost vindictive effeminacy. 'Say, why don't you come on down?' he added in a more normal tone.

'You *can* see him from where you're phoning?'

'Well, I can't actually see him from here, but he's there all right. He's at the bar.'

'Bad business! Listen, I'm coming down there. Now, you cover him. Get a line on him. If he leaves before I arrive, stay with him — *tail* him, eh? Contact me, at first opportunity, there at the bar. I'll wait there for your call. Do you have it?'

'Right.'

'Get yourself a vantage point — as unobtrusive as possible. When I arrive, I'll sit beside you, but we won't exchange any sign of recognition. Do you understand?'

'Okay, when are you coming?'

'I'll leave at once. I'll be there within the quarter-hour.'

'Okay.'

'Very well then . . . Now, you're doing a good job, Frost. Things are looking up. We may break this case sooner than you think.'

'I'll see you here then,' said Frost in a heavy swallow. He had evidently taken his drink with him into the phone booth.

'Right you are,' said Fred Eichner.

— and several were, presenting now a sort of panelled wall, exuding through its openings at the top the flickering glow of candlelight that often patterned the ceiling with wavering, fragmentary shadows of those inside the booths.

Beneath the gradually burdening echo of music from the farther dining room, a current of treble and breathless laughter fled round the bar, flippantly spurred by the tinkles of stirring rods on icy glass.

There was a formal uneasiness about the carefully dressed people at the bar. From all appearances, about half of them were pretending to be smugly sinister, and the other half, desperately, not to notice. It was transparent, however, that the men were there through a deep, innocent nervousness, and the women, too, because of it.

Martin Frost struck a garish contrast with this setting. When Dr Eichner entered, he saw Frost immediately, leaning across the bar. Sloven, in his unpressed suit, talking to one of the three tight-lipped waiters, he looked like a rumpled giant.

The Doctor had prepared a perfect countenance of detachment for the situation, but this was smashed when Frost turned his half closed-eyed face fully toward him and, without changing his position across the bar, said in a loud voice: 'How ya' *keeping,*' Doc?' Evidently, he had been drinking quite heavily, for even before the Doctor reached him he spoke out again: 'How you keepin', Doc?'

'Hello,' said Dr Eichner evenly. He could not yet be sure that Frost wasn't putting on a strategic act.

'What'll you have, Doc?' Frost was speaking much too loud, and several people were forced to glance caustically in his direction, concealing their embarrassment beneath looks of cynical amusement.

'Eh? Oh, martini for me, please.'

'Double martini for Doc Fred Eichner!' said Frost, bringing his hand down flat on the bar, but soft enough not to make any sound.

'Take it easy, pal,' the bartender said, not looking directly at Frost.

Frost opened his eyes very wide, slowly exaggerating an expression of surprise at the bartender who had begun to wipe vigorously over an unseen spot on the bar. Frost addressed him in a dramatic stage-whisper. 'Right!' he agreed. 'And do you know *why*? Come here, eh?' His enunciation was crisp now and, seeming perfectly sober, he winked at the bartender and took him by the wrist, gently but firmly pulling him closer, raising himself on his stool as he did. 'Because *easy-does-it*! Eh? Ha! Ha ha ha!' And, as he spoke, he lifted the shot-glass he held in his other hand and cracked it from top to bottom in a slow, one-finger squeeze.

'Double martini for Fred Eichner' he concluded, reverting with a heavy frown, to his drunkenness.

At just that moment, two people left the booth directly behind them. Indicating the empty space there with a the room, while Frost smiled sheepishly into his own fresh drink. There was no sign of Mr Treevly.

The Doctor had withheld speaking to Frost, waiting for a cue from him. When it was not forthcoming, however, and Frost — even though it was apparent that he was not being observed now by anyone other than Eichner himself — continued to look almost happily lost, nodding and humming low, the Doctor was forced to bring matters to a point. 'Well?' he demanded in a whisper.

It was evidently what Frost had been waiting for, since now he beamed modestly and, raising a circled finger of confidence, he winked slyly at Fred Eichner. 'In-the-bag!' he said.

The Doctor carefully closed the doors of the booth. 'Where is he?'

'He isn't here now, he left while I was on the phone.'

'Bad business!' snapped Eichner.

'No, wait,' said Frost, looking very earnest, but quite drunk now. 'Wait. I've got a line on this guy, Doc. You see, I *know* where he is.'

Dr Eichner drank about half his martini, showing his impatience. 'Go ahead.'

'Well, what time is it?'

'Twelve minutes after seven.'

'Good! Good. Now, listen. Treevly — *and* his friend —

are going to be at a TV broadcast at eight o'clock, a studio broadcast—and, so-are-we! Eh?' He downed his drink in a gulp.

'You're sure about that,' said the Doctor sternly.

'It cost us a fiver,' said Frost loudly, 'but I'm-as-sure as you're . . . Doc-tor Freddie Eichner! Eh? Haw! Ha Ha ha!'

'Lower your voice,' said Eichner. 'There's no advantage in drawing attention to ourselves at this point.' He eyed Frost critically. 'You seem to be intoxicated. Are you aware of that?'

Before the other could reply, there was a discreet knock at the door of the booth, almost a scratching, and a girl's soft voice, 'Marty, Marty . . .' Martin opened the door to a well-dressed, animated young blonde who kept glancing from the booth to the people seated behind her. Dr Eichner noticed that almost everyone in sight was watching their booth.

'Doc, I want you to meet one of the sweetest little ladies in the business. Jean-baby, this is Doc Fred Eichner.'

'How do you do,' said the Doctor, half rising.

'Have a seat, Jean-baby, take a load-off,' Frost went on, lolling his great drunken head.

The girl laughed engagingly. She had an extremely small, insect-like face, tapered above by blonde hair, neatly piled in a sort of bullet-shape. She sat down by Dr Eichner, immediately very close. Frost closed the booth doors, but, before doing so, he dramatically shook his fist at the people sitting nearby.

'Take it easy, Marty,' the girl cautioned, laying a hand on his wrist, then at once turned her smiling attention to

'Low cars and high women,' he replied dryly, rising to the spirit of the talk.

'Hey, this is no hick,' cried Jean-baby with an air of serious discovery; and, for emphasis, she insistently nudged Frost's arm. 'This is no cornball hick!' She looked avidly from one man to the other.

Frost nodded, but addressed his remark, quite soberly, to the Doctor. 'She is an acquaintance of you-know-who.'

Fred Eichner returned the nod and waxed sage behind the glass he raised to the girl.

'No secrets, Marty!' she snapped, instinctively touching the purse in her lap. 'Keep it clean, or count me out!' For an instant she expressed a sullen self-pity, then turned spritely again to the Doctor. 'You're no hick, Doc, I can tell you *that*. Say! Gin-flips all around! My treat!'

Dr Eichner started to object, but Frost caught his eye with a scathing frown, and the girl was allowed to proceed. 'Grade-A all around, Tony,' she called through the closed door. 'Three slops for three slobs, eh Doc?' She gave him a sultry-lidded wink, and while they waited for the drinks, further engaged the Doctor's attention by producing harsh sounds to accompany the music that drifted in from the dining room, all the while dreamily seeking his eyes and swaying slightly as though she were dancing. Beside her, the Doctor sipped his Martini in restrained anticipation, though, apparently, it was not yet propitious to bring the talk around to Treevly, as Frost, opposite, stared contemplatively down into his empty shot-glass, even a little morosely it would seem.

When the drinks arrived, Jean-baby set them in a row in front of her and, leaning cautiously forward, took a sip or two from each white brimmed glass, leaving a trace of lipstick on the rims which she wiped off in turn with a twist of her thumb and forefinger. Then, bringing her purse up on the table, she opened it and took out a household can of ground nutmeg, and a pencil. She proceeded to empty the contents of the can proportionately into each glass, stirring with the pencil as she did.

An instant after this operation had begun, Dr Eichner, obviously troubled, looked to Frost for a cue, whereupon the latter winked with solemn confidence and nodded to affirm it.

When the nutmeg had been stirred in, Jean-baby passed the drinks around. 'Here you are, Doc,' she said genially, 'this will give that funny old mind of yours something to think about.'

'Thank you,' said the Doctor and raised his glass in a silent toast, but not to his lips until Frost and Jean-baby had begun to drink.

Frost made no effort to conceal his distaste for the drink, but took it down in one long draught, grimacing the while. Jean-baby stopped from time to time to stir hers with the pencil, which she handed to the Doctor.

'It won't dissolve, see, so you have to get it before it settles on the bottom.'

'I understand,' said Dr Eichner, following suit. 'Nut-

I understand you to say *hash-ish*? the Indian hemp?' He looked to Frost for an explanation, but none was forthcoming as the other had lapsed into preoccupation once more. 'Why, that's Cannabis, the Indian hemp!' He peered intently down into his glass, as though his keen eyes would make an exacting analysis of the residue there. 'Hash-ish and nutmeg!'

'You've got to get with it, Doc,' announced Frost, suddenly recovering. 'Let's drink up.' He ordered another round, a shot for himself, a Pink Lady for Jean-baby, and a double Martini for the Doctor.

No sooner had the drinks arrived than Frost demanded to know the time. It was a quarter to eight. He hurriedly downed his drink and indicated that the Doctor, too, should drink up. 'O.K.' said Frost, standing abruptly, 'let's get moving,' and, opening the door, he stepped out of the booth and fell squarely face down on the carpeted floor. It caused a great commotion in the bar, and before the Doctor could reach him, two of the waiters were on their knees, hovering over the body.

'No interference here,' said Dr Eichner, waving them back, 'I'm a physician.'

For a moment, Frost was evidently unconscious, but he quickly came to, and then got to his feet with no trouble at all.

'Let's get moving,' he said tersely to Fred Eichner. His eyes held a slight, troubled glaze, but his speech was plain and unhurried.

'Take it easy, Marty,' said Jean-baby who had also gotten up and had put her hand on Dr Eichner's shoulder, though Fred Eichner, in helping Frost to his feet, showed a certain unsteadiness himself. He was evidently confounded, too, by Frost's apparent condition.

'Are you coming with us?' he asked then, turning to Jean-baby, dully hoping to bring the talk around to Treevly.

'We'll be seeing her later,' Frost put in before the girl could answer, 'here, at the bar.' And taking the Doctor's arm, he started for the door.

Jean-baby smiled agreement at them both, raising her Pink Lady in salute, and sat down at the bar as Dr Eichner and the private detective began to mechanically thread their way between the high bar-stools and the tables of upraised faces, toward the door, and out.

CHAPTER XVI

EVEN at not yet quite eight, the street outside the Mayfair, by contrast with sick-soft interior behind them, was dancing with the sunlight of late afternoon, and the two men momentarily shielded their eyes against it.

'This way,' said Frost, asserting a dramatic pressure

[illegible] to Frost for a reaction, but the latter, plodding oblivious beside him, seemed not even to hear, and the Doctor continued, 'I mean, since nothing was gained by it, nothing tangible at least, in terms of our — our purpose at the Mayfair. Do you follow my meaning, Frost?' he insisted then, touching Frost's arm, and the great hulk shrugged. 'Why live in the past?' he answered finally, with considerable effort, whereupon Dr Eichner fell silent again and they walked on, with a solemn intentness that somehow set them apart from the rest of the casual side-walk-traffic.

'A moment ago,' Dr Eichner resumed almost at once, 'you inferred the futility of deprecating the past — futility of remorse, or rather that the *immediate* negative approach — or *that* approach to what is immediate . . . A point well taken —' They had reached an intersection then, and Dr Eichner broke off his speech, as though nothing more could be accomplished until the light changed.

An attractive, unescorted girl beside them gave the pair a glance of defiant nonchalance which, when they failed to respond, became a look of suspicion, and, finally, of rude disdain. She marched rapidly ahead as the light went green.

'Nutmeg,' the Doctor took it up again as they started

across behind her, 'contains at least one serious alkaloid —and the effects of Indian hemp are well known. My point is this: our general perspective, our sense of—of values, so to speak, may undergo a change—a decided change which we might fail to take into account—to calibrate—*unless*, this is my point, we are prepared to take this, or such a change—*into* account! Now. Now then—'

Frost came to a sudden halt, drawing the Doctor up short beside him. They had reached the Studio and were standing opposite, just across the street from it. From here, the cream stucco building could have resembled almost any large, modern cinema, but, by the restraint of its marquee, it seemed somehow more respectable, like an institution; and on the sidewalk adjacent it, an orderly double-file stretch of people was in movement toward the entrance.

'There,' said Frost, moving his head in an indicative gesture toward the file, whereupon Dr Eichner, after staring at Frost for an instant in incomprehension, followed his eye and got a vivid glimpse of Treevly, in lively converse with his friend, moving at the fore.

'Ah, yes,' said the Doctor softly, making a wry face, as with a swallow of strong, vintage brandy. 'There, indeed.' The line of people was moving easily and, as he watched, Treevly and his companion rounded the corner, out of sight, into the Studio lobby.

'Come on,' said Fred Eichner, 'and keep a sharp lookout.' They soberly crossed the street and joined the diminishing file, attracting the notice, with their intense repose, of everyone nearby.

[illegible], looking keenly about, craning his head at the marquee above. 'What's being presented? I know very little about video.' But they had already passed too far beneath the marquee and, even now, were turning into the carpeted foyer of the Studio—where there was as yet, by sign or token, no evidence of what was in store—and the Doctor had suddenly become quite nervously, buoyantly alert to things. 'Eh? What's the nature of it, Frost? What's it to be?'

'*Quiz-show,*' Frost managed at last, his words now as thick and heavy as doom itself.

CHAPTER XVII

THIS studio-auditorium is quite large and, as such places go, comfortable enough.

Dr Eichner and Frost were admitted without difficulty and took two of the few remaining seats near the back. The studio audience was at capacity and in a gala mood; apparently, some phase of the entertainment was already under way. On stage, or rather, in the studio proper—

situated dead ahead on a slightly higher level than the audience, and weighted to the right by the glassed control-booth—obvious last-minute preparations were at hand. Five heavy chairs at a large forum-table was the centre of things, while all around them great cameras and microphones were being shifted and given final adjustment by men in shirt sleeves. At the table, each place was set with an ashtray, a drinking glass, and a small decanter of water, which were checked and rearranged from time to time.

The audience, meanwhile, was not idle but engaged in clamorous exchange with a well-dressed young man standing at a microphone near the first row of seats on the left. He encouraged their response by laughing a great deal and leaning forward with broad winks and grimaces. He spoke in an unusually loud voice, almost shouting.

'Say, I think we're going to have a lot of fun here tonight! Come to think of it, we *always* have a lot of fun here, don't we?'

He beamed fanatically and cupped one hand to his ear in an exaggerated attempt to hear the audience's reply.

'Yes!' they cried.

'I mean, DON'T WE?'

'YES!'

At this, Dr Eichner, who had been unobtrusively scanning the rows ahead for a sight of Treevly, sat bolt upright in his chair, stunned and confused by the roaring crowd. He was on the verge of appealing to Frost when, suddenly he caught sight of Treevly, sitting at the end of a row very near the front. The Doctor immediately reached into the inside pocket of his coat to withdraw a

audience re-
sponse, Treevly would cup both hands to his mouth, and apparently join in at the top of his voice, while his companion watched him with evident admiration, glancing around animatedly from moment to moment to get the reaction of those nearby. Then Treevly would face him again and the two of them would laugh riotously, exchanging looks of merriment with their neighbours. It was obvious that the pair were great favourites at the studio.

Dr Eichner continued to scrutinize them through his glasses, making several side remarks to Frost without turning his head—so that he failed to notice the glazed lethargy that had come over the latter, slumped forward in his chair eyes seemingly focussed on the back of the person in front of him. However, just as the Doctor was about to force the glasses on Frost, a loud buzzing resounded through the Studio, signifying that the programme would be on the air immediately. The young man at the microphone dramatically raised his hands, so that the show opened on a sea of hushed titters and coughings. Then he did a spectacular, backward-somersault terminating in a French split, at which the audience roared, and turning around he presented the host, a rotund, proudly self-effacing man who came striding jovially on stage at that instant.

The programme, as it developed, was a popular radio

and TV quiz-show, called 'What's My Disease?' and the host, who served as moderator to the panel, introduced its four members as they ceremoniously entered and took up their places at the table: a prominent woman columnist, a professional football coach, an actress, and a professor of Logic from the University of Chicago. The panel members were good-naturedly jibed by the moderator, and they smiled a great deal in return. They seldom looked directly at the audience, but rather at the moderator who assured their constant liaison with the audience by continually turning his glance from them to the panel members and back again, always with a show of serious goodwill.

After a moment's distraction, Dr Eichner re-trained his glasses on Treevly, and was only vaguely aware of the other developments going forward as the moderator took his place at the end of the table and the first contestant was brought in. The contestant could not be seen, but was wheeled in, completely obscured in a sort of raised, shrouded cage.

'Can you speak?' asked the moderator.

'Yes,' was the muted reply.

'All right, panel.'

The first questions proceeded rapidly, suggesting, by their tone a tediously familiar pattern.

'Local or general?' asked the football coach.

'Local.'

'Manifestations visible?' asked the woman columnist.

'Oh, yes.'

'Is it—your face?' asked the actress, taking a flyer.

'No.'

[illegible] seemed
[illegible], even blushing a little.

'Are these manifestations,' began the Professor, raising his voice to be heard, 'above, or below, the waist-line?'

'Below.'

'Is it of the limbs?' he continued.

The answer was hesitant. '— Yes.'

'A *single* limb?' the Professor hurried, hard on the scent of it now, as the moderator beamed knowingly and the rest of the panel began to smile in anticipation.

'Yes.'

'*Is* it elephantiasis?' demanded the Professor.

'Yes.'

The moderator took up the triumph quickly, and with grand good humour. 'Yes, it IS *elephantiasis*!' and at that moment, as the shroud was dropped and the contestant revealed to them all, the audience took in its breath as one in a great audible gasp of astonished horror, and then burst into applause for the Professor, the contestant, the moderator, and the whole panel, while the latter exchanged informal congratulatory gestures all around, the actress especially animated in showing her modest appreciation of their victory.

'What's going on here?' demanded Dr Eichner, suddenly irate, of Frost, as the questioning of the second contestant moved underway. Frost, however, sitting like the leaning Buddha he resembled, seemed now to have lost consciousness, though his eyes remained partially open and he was in no apparent danger of falling off the chair. The Doctor turned his glasses onto the panel and scrutinized the proceedings there, muttering inaudible asides as the questions and answers went forward:

'Is your condition local, or general?'

'General.'

'Are the manifestations of this condition *visible*?'

'And how!'

This brought a laugh from the audience, and tolerant smiles from some of the panel. The actress, however whose turn it was, remained darkly serious. 'Is it your face—' she began, but was brought up short by the woman columnist who reminded her with quiet firmness: *'General.'*

'Oh, yes, well, it wouldn't be that then—thank goodness!' and she turned a winning smile to the audience, who murmured accord. Then she seemed at a loss for the moment.

'Can you talk?' she blurted.

'Well—'

The audience roared, but with forgiving good nature.

'No, I mean, can you *walk*?'

'Oh, yes.'

The actress gave a sigh of relief and let the questioning pass on.

'Is there pain . . . generally?' asked the football coach, raising one eyebrow.

'No-oo'

'Is this a progressive condition?' demanded the Professor.

panel with his glasses.

Meanwhile, things were coming to a head on stage.

'You *did* say "scales?" '

'Yes.'

A murmur of consternation in the audience.

'Is it Icthyosis?' ventured the woman columnist.

'Yes!'

'Yes, it IS *Icthyosis*!'

The covering was removed with a flourish, and the crowd gave their customary gasp of repulsion, and then burst into applause.

On the wall behind the panel, like a backdrop for a stage of players, was a large board of multi-coloured lights depicting the human body's interior. This board was evidently connected with an electric audio-response device, so that the lights reacted to sound—blinking and brightening as the volume and rapidity of speech, laughter, whistling, etc. increased in the studio. As the questioning became faster and more enthusiastic, the anatomy of lights would intensify, becoming brighter and brighter, until, after making a peculiar wavering glow when the audience took in its breath at the unveiling of the contestant, it would flash into climax with their final burst of applause, shuddering and raging with intolerable brightness for fully half a minute. Then it would die down and glow, faintly pulsating at each question and response as they got under way again, to build once more to the very end.

'Goitre-colussi?'

'No. No, it isn't Goitre-col—'

'*Multiple*-Goitre!'

'*Multiple*-Goitre . . . it is! It *is* Multiple-Goitre!'

'Oooooooooooooooooooooh!'

And as the crowd abandoned itself to cheering applause, the board of lights burned and throbbed as though they had been short-circuited. The strange radiance of colour and refraction given off by the board caused the faces in the audience to appear separately stark and isolate, and often rather distorted.

'It isn't . . . . *Giant Measle*?'

'Yes! It is! It's GIANT MEASLE!'

'Bah' shuddered the Doctor angrily; he began to scan the audience with his glasses. 'I'm clearing out, Frost,' he said in a terse shout. 'Keep your man covered and contact me—back at the Mayfair.' So saying he stalked unsteadily out of the Studio, waving aside the protests of the door-guard, and leaving behind Frost, whose face now reminded one somehow of nothing so much as cold, polished stone.

Ralph was preparing two whisky-and-cokes into paper cups he had just produced from the glove compartment.

'Be prepared, that's our motto,' said Babs brightly. The darling girl was beaming; Ralph had suggested that after the film they go to Monsieur Croque, a dapper supper-club on Sunset Strip. And, for the occasion, Babs had worn her smartest black shantung, simple but not severe, a clever dress with a thin, gleaming line of pink-pearl buttons that parted her breasts like a smouldering arrow. Her hair was caught back with two small combs, leaving a vibrant white length of throat, which she managed to arch with becoming defiance, feeling the pulse of it beneath stretched sinews. At first glance, on the fleeting instants when her face was in repose, she might have resembled the ingenue of some deadly-chic Lesbian set, but under this polished veneer the girl felt herself all vulnerably rounded warmths of satin and lace.

'Well, here's to it,' she said, looking mischievous as she raised her cup.

'Here's to the *ladies*,' Ralph countered, '—bottoms up!'

Babs made a face of disapproval, first in mock reprimand to shame Ralph's toast, and then in earnest distaste for the drink in her hand.

'Uh-uh,' she said significantly, shaking her head and

returning the almost full cup. 'No, thank you! More *coke* for me, please.'

Ralph posed a look of quizzical reproach at her as he added more coke to the cup, while Babs, in her turn, seemed to withdraw genteelly towards her side of the car and, as though she might be placing the boy on probation, actually started looking at the distant screen, where, at the moment, a two-weeks old newsreel was on view. While they sat in relative silence—for Ralph had shut down the small amplifier the attendant had attached to their window—as one of hundreds of couples, each housed separately dark within the vast parking lot, seeing the stale, mute heartbreaks of world news, it gradually started raining.

Ralph rolled his window part way up and, seeing that Babs was having difficulty with hers, leaned over to help her, kissing her lightly on the temple as he did.

'Oh, it's going to rain!' said Babs crossly, unmoved by his attention. 'And I didn't bring a *scarf*! Oh, how awful!'

'Oh, I don't know,' said Ralph, 'maybe it will be nice.' He cheerfully made some adjustments inside the car, touching the cloth top here and there, and closing the hood ventilator. He turned on the radio and found some soft music, while Babs looked on hopelessly. Under the varying refractions of light from the screen and the radio dial, her still face did like a marvellously sculptured thing in certain half-lights, taking on qualities of beauty that were at once permanent and elusive; and her eyes seemed to contain little pieces of fire.

'But I don't have *anything*,' she announced, '*for my head*!'

[illegible], and when Babs—cautious in attempting to negotiate it with the drink in her hand—started to hand the cup to him, he quickly urged her to finish it up, which could have, as an emergency measure, seemed feasible enough, for the boy had both hands occupied himself—one pulling back the seat, the other holding his own cup—and so, she did it. She downed it in one grimaced-draught, but seemed quite pleased and happy with herself at once, as though it were, under the circumstances, a justifiable lark. And a minute later they were snugly together in the back seat, where everything was darker and somehow suggestive of absolute seclusion; and, as Ralph prepared their drinks again, 'Wuthering Heights' opened on the far screen ahead, its images broken, like those in a dream, by the rivulets of rain that cut a patternless criss-cross over the windshield, while much closer at hand, the soft-glowing radio played 'Mood Indigo.'

'Do you like to dance?' asked Ralph, ignoring the film.

'Um. Love it,' said Babs softly, looking straight ahead.

He took her hand and held it gingerly. She seemed to accept this as part of seeing the movie, but then she looked at him once, briefly, smiling some sort of insinuating reproach, and nodded toward the screen.

Ralph, his eyes never leaving her face, put his other arm on the seat behind her and, in a moment, leaned over to kiss her mouth, but the girl turned away and drew back a little, so he kissed her cheek instead, which she allowed him to do, lightly. 'I love you,' he said tenderly, and she turned her great eyes toward him with their expression of slow amazement.

And when Ralph looked into the eyes it *was* almost lovingly. Then, with violent abruptness, he dropped his arm around her shoulders like a vice and pulled the girl to him, taking her chin in his left hand and kissing her mouth so hard and surely that she could only whimper through clenched teeth. Babs struck out in genuine terror at the hand holding her face, but Ralph, using the arm that encircled her, seized the defending hand from behind and held it fast by the wrist.

By the sudden initial movement, Ralph had pinioned the girl's left arm between them, so that, with both arms restrained and her face held tightly, Babs was utterly helpless. Her mouth went vibrantly rigid beneath his and her whole frame shuddered against him like someone convulsing in a straight-jacket: she was able to do nothing but writhe and kick with her knees, which she did, in savage desperation, but only for a moment, then she fell limp in hopeless exhaustion as the boy kissed her long and hard, moving his mouth around over hers, probingly, working his fingers into her cheeks, trying to unlock the teeth, as one might to give a kitten medicine.

Ralph's right arm was around Babs' neck and shoulders and with that hand he held her own right back by the wrist, holding it next to her head while, with the fingers he fondled her ear and hair-line. But she would not part the teeth, and yet her eyes were closed now—almost leased it, and the girl unhesitatingly threw that arm around his neck, thrusting herself to him, as if with a so much fiercer need than his own, that he at once dropped his other hand from her face to her nearest breast. Babs twisted her face sharply away, at the same time withdrawing her arm from around him to grasp the terrible hand.

'Please,' she begged and turned to look at the boy imploringly, but he immediately regained the former advantage, seizing her face and hand, kissing her mouth deeply for a full minute, and when she responded this time and he lowered his hand to her blouse, he did not release the wrist, and the only thing she could do was tear her mouth from him again.

'Ralph, please. *Please*. You're hurting my arm!' She sounded on the verge of panic and tears, and—her face being turned away—the boy kissed her neck and ears, whispering mournfully, 'Babs, I love you so,' undoing, as he spoke, the central six buttons of her blouse, wherein he entered his hand caressingly.

'*No*. No, no,' she pleaded, and the convulsions began anew, struggling to get her impossible left arm from between them, accompanied by fearful sobs now that her mouth was uncovered. But Ralph held fast, and by gradually closing the arm that encircled her, brought her head toward his own, and managed to slowly turn the face with her own hand, which as we know, he held vice-like at the wrist against her cheek. Babs exerted her fullest to prevent this, and, for a moment, actually seemed to forget her anxiety in the sheer contest of physical power it appeared to be — *appeared*, because the boy managed it so slowly, as though strategically prolonging the drain of strength and energy as might otherwise stand her in good stead at the later, more crucial stages of thwarting their love. During this tedious manoeuvre, of narrowing the space between their heads, Babs' face contorted grotesquely with strains and grimaces of hopeful effort, but for the last few inches it became all hushed and closed-eyed again, as, in the illusion of having had a chance, she had once more exhausted herself completely, and honourably lost, was again buried in kisses.

Meanwhile, Ralph's other hand had not been idle, though it only lay carefully inside the blouse, over the lace-wrought bosom, which he caressed gently, almost soothingly, as if not to frighten the dear sparrow-thing huddled there, waiting until his mouth covered hers again before attempting the filigreed nest itself — which he did, at last, with steely tenderness. This new effort, however, was met with an outburst of actual tears, even though, or perhaps because, it succeeded. The girl sobbed up through the kisses wet and piteously, her body going limp and lifeless again, except for the mouth with tremored softly as she cried, while Ralph kissed her — her cheeks and her eyes — with great, real lovingness.

'Ralph . . . please don't. Oh, please, please, please . . .'

'Don't cry, Babs,' he whispered. 'Please don't cry. I love

She shook her head blindly, sobbing. 'No! No, no!'

'Please, darling, I love you so much.'

'No, I can't, I can't. Please STOP...'

But when he kissed her again, violently on the mouth, and released both of her arms, she flung them round his neck, and it was as if she wanted to do nothing so much as eat him alive. She pressed against him furiously, and Ralph, very gradually, gave way, even pulling a little, until their bodies were leaning at something like a 45° angle to the seat, completely off balance, in favour of reclining, at which point he allowed them to fall, though slowly, at the same time turning Babs clockwise by the shoulders, so that she was, at the end of this manoeuvre, on the inside of the seat, with her back to its wall, so to speak.

This was a transition of which Babs, lost in kisses, seemed fervidly oblivious—until Ralph's left hand abandoned the bosom for the pelvic region, a move which touched off, like a hair-triggered device, a phase of unparalleled outrage and frantic defence. But the girl was even more securely bridled than before, under the additional handicap now of Ralph's partial weight upon her. And except that their embrace was now more or less horizontal, their positions had remained exactly the same, with Bab's left arm being half under and on the other side of him, and, of course, hopelessly out of it, while her right was still locked at the wrist by his own right which encircled her shoulders and held her fast against him.

Writhing and convulsing, she sobbed great pleas up through the kisses, and seemed so on the verge of some sort of internal explosion, that Ralph released, almost as a gift, her right hand, which immediately seized his own left and tried desperately to undo its maddening design, whereupon Ralph's right hand was at once lowered into the shattered arrow of Bab's dress-front, and the girl was able to wrench her mouth from his, crying, 'Ralph, oh please, Ralph please, oh Ralph.'

And he, woefully : 'Oh Babs, I love you so much. Babs, I love you so.'

But Babs was too near hysteria for romantic talk. She suddenly made her voice perversely calm, trying to sound reasonable, yet with a good deal of warmth and promise, too. 'Ralph, let's stop for a few minutes, please, just for a minute, please, darling, please . . .' at which point he kissed her deeply in the ear, and along the neck; and she, almost as in a fit, snatched the hand at her breast and tried to bite it, at the same time bursting into tears again.

Ralph withdrew his hand from her bosom and returned it to her face, which he held again for kissing; and then he raised the pelvic hand as well, using it now to stroke her hair and face as he kissed her, soothingly, saying : 'Don't be afraid, darling. I love you so much, please don't be afraid,' and he put both arms around her in gentle closeness, calming her wondrously, as he allowed his left hand to go lovingly down her side and over to her knees, [illegible] until the hand did reach the point where she burst into tears as if now and never really before her heart-of-hearts was surely broken. But the hand was there, so searchingly, findingly, undeniably there. 'Oh no Ralph darling please no Ralph please I love you so, please don't Ralph oh please stop please oh please please please please PLEASE STOP Ralph please oh please Ralph God please stop please God make him stop I can't stand it RALPH oh please oh *I'm going to scream*! Ralph I will oh please I will scream Ralph I will! I will!'

And Ralph did stop, moaning, 'Please, Babs, please, darling, kiss me, Babs, I love you so much.' And she kissed him insanely, half in gratitude for his having stopped, and half in raging hunger, as he, left hand resting quietly on the top part of her leg, gently undid the stocking-hooks.

'Please don't be afraid, Babs, darling,' he said, returning his hand inside, and easing one knee between her own. 'You know I love you so much, Babs, please, I love you so.'

'No, Ralph, not any more, please, not now, Ralph, please listen, Ralph, not here, please, let's wait, really, Ralph, darling, please, no really please, oh Ralph I love you please don't, really don't please Ralph I can't darling I love you please, oh Ralph, please, I can't Ralph you don't know please I'd rather die please God oh please God Ralph you're hurting me please oh no please oh no oh please no . . .'

During the final crucial assault, Babs, let it be said for the darling girl, comported herself like a thing possessed, creature-like, threatening to bite and scratch the boy, and though, never actually going quite so far as that, did fight with an otherwise frenetic desperation until the last lace-edged line of defence was breached aside, and even then, when all strength had deserted her and she was incapable of further effort, she still imagined herself, for a time, to be resisting.

Finally, however, she felt herself yielding to rest, as though one part of her were outside, disinterestedly watching, while another part of her stayed in so far inside herself that everything was in a sort of soft-focus blur where the only reality was a gnawing want and, finally, a pain. And then she clasped him and the tearing pain to her viciously, as though this had suddenly become the last, or first, touch with dear life; and as she felt the proverbial wings of the great moth spread upward flexing within her, carrying the myth of reality and a part of awareness up and away, the moth grew to the size of some great winged bird, chained to the bottom of a vat of champagne, moving his wings with powerful, majestic slowness, and the bubbles rose on every side, streaming in deathless, thrilling flights to nowhere.

'Oh Ralph,' she breathed, worshipfully, '*Ralph.*'

'How was it, Doc?' asked the girl as soon as they were seated in the booth.

'What's that!' said Eichner crossly. A searing ache had moved in behind his eyes, making it difficult for him to focus his attention, and he had suddenly become so suspicious of his surroundings, that he felt a desperate want of time.

'Well, the broadcast, how was it? Where's Marty?'

The Doctor took his head in both hands. 'Why do you ask?'

Jean-baby didn't bother to reply. 'You're cute,' she said a second later, and gave his wrist a pinch that made him start.

'I can't discuss it with you now,' said Eichner, ignoring her gesture momentarily, but then shrugged his shoulders helplessly. 'My—my head hurts.' This note of child-like apology may have struck some remote maternal device inside the girl, for she laughed with soft embarrassment and touched his temple slightly.

'Too much hemp,' said the Doctor vaguely, trying to explain. 'Too-much-hemp.'

'Yes,' she keened, not comprehending, 'yes, yes,' stroking his bent head. And, in less than a minute, he was asleep and slowly easing his head down to the table and forward on cradling arms.

At that moment someone entered the bar and Jean-baby raised her eyes to see Frost glide past the booth like a zombie.

'*Here* Marty!' she said brightly, reaching out for him with one arm while with the other giving Fred Eichner a sharp nudge. 'Come on, Doc, join the party!'

Frost turned and, after staring at them sat down opposite. For a moment he seemed strangely detached.

'Fred Eichner, is it?' he asked, frowning over the great inert head. 'Well, we've got to get cracking. Something's up. Bring him around.'

'Let him snort some schmeck!' said Jean-baby, wide-eyed, reaching for her purse.

'No, no,' said Frost irritably. 'Get pepper.' He looked toward the bar for a waiter.

'Pepper?' asked Jean. 'What's the kick? What kind of pepper?'

'Ordinary pepper, of course,' said Frost. 'Black pepper.'

'What's it have in it, black pepper?' but Frost didn't seem to be listening. Looking toward the bar, his face had contorted into a grimace of extraordinary annoyance.

'Pepper here!' he said loudly. 'Black pepper here!'

'Cool it, Marty,' said Jean-baby. 'I'll make the run.' She appeared dramatically apprehensive as she rose and went towards the rear of the bar, but she was back very soon, all smiles.

'Marty, the score's set — and here's the stash!'

She put a small can of black pepper down on the table in front of him.

said Frost, 'and cut that hipster gab. It's making me sick.'

Jean thoughtfully transferred the pile of black pepper to Frost's hand, even lightly tapping the back of her own to free the clinging fragments.

'How do you make it?' she demanded, watching Frost intently.

'Like this,' said Frost, and with an abrupt little movement he flung the handful of pepper on the table under the Doctor's face.

It had the effect of some sort of unusual personnel bomb in that the Doctor went abruptly upright in an explosion of sneezes and coughs.

'Steady on,' said Frost, putting out a hand to detain the Doctor when he started to rise.

'Wow!' marvelled Jean-baby, 'what a flash!' She was watching them both very closely now, really impressed.

'Something's up, Doc,' said Frost. 'We've got to get cracking.'

Eichner looked terrible. Eyes all red and streaming, his face seemed caught up in a kind of permanent twist of wrath and anxiety. He tried to speak but only made a gurgling sound.

Jean-baby sat gazing at the box in her hand, in complete wonder over the simple phenomenon.

'Wow,' she mused, 'it must be the end groove kick!' And suddenly she put her own head down on the table the way Fred Eichner's had been, closing her eyes and pushing the can toward Frost. 'Go!' she said. 'Make it!'

'Will you shut up,' said Frost, that impatient with her now. 'Something's up, Fred,' he went on in even tones to the Doctor. 'Do you follow me?'

Dr Eichner continued to stare at him, horror-stricken and seemingly with no comprehension at all, but he nodded his head rather oddly to show understanding, and Frost continued, leaning forward in confidence. 'A trap,' he said softly. 'A trap for Treevly.'

Dr Eichner nodded again, this time making a funny little effort to wax sage as well.

'Here's the set-up,' said Frost, taking out a very small address book and gesturing with it to make points of emphasis. 'After the broadcast, I got talking to Treevly—and his friend, and I invited them to a *party*. At your place! Tonight. They'll be there in an hour. We've got to get cracking.'

'I'll get the chicks—you get the lush!' cried Jean shrilly. Marty's got-a-party and

a trap for *Treev-ly*!'

'All right, cool it!' said Frost to the girl. 'Get a couple of interesting chicks, and let's make it.'

'What about a hashish and peyote buffet?' asked Jean. 'I'll make the run.'

Frost frowned heavily at first, then seemed to consider it, tapping the address book against his open hand. 'Hmm. Make it look like a real party, eh? Hmm, I wonder.' He of the address book. 'Be there in half-an-hour, and no slip-ups!'

'Right Marty!' said Jean, smart in her attempt at efficiency, but getting to her feet rather jerkily.

The minute she was gone, Frost ordered up.

'We'll slap down a couple of hard ones, then we'll be getting this show on the road, Fred.'

Dr Eichner, passing a hand slowly across his eyes, didn't speak but appeared to be following Frost's words more easily now.

CHAPTER XX

BY THE time Frost and Fred Eichner reached the Doctor's home in Lord's Canyon, it was evident, even as they ascended the drive, that a party of sorts was already under way. Strains of soft music wafted across the wide lawn from the house, and girl-sounds as well, all tinkles and laughter.

'Good,' said Frost as he assisted Dr Eichner on the steps, 'Jean's set it up nicely.'

The Doctor's house was a large and pleasant one—

white colonial with great French windows fronting the wide-terraced grounds.

Stretched the long full face of the house was one wide unbroken room, a sweep of greyed-pearl elegance; a spatial room, delicately poised, yet hushed and restful, with ebony, cream, or satin-wood appointments and a blackening-red portrait or two on the farther walls. Opening from one corner of this room where the guests moved about as in an underwater ballet, was the half-closed door of a darkened study, seen rich and cozy by the soft blazing grate that played rose-blue firelight in tints of gold across panelled walls and the malt, blood, and moss coloured tomes of vellum and suede.

Upon entering, the doctor seemed to recover himself momentarily and, with the manner of a man suddenly aware of his position as host, began moving about the room wanting to see to all things at once. The guests, however, appeared already comfortably engaged. Jean had brought along three other young girls, and two of them caressed in slowly viscous dance, in the centre of the room, while the third swayed alone nearby in closed-eyed langour, to a dripping saxophone's 'Indian Love Call.'

Jean-baby herself was active at the sideboard, preparing more canapes from the hashish-candy, mah-joong, and peyote-paste — the latter which she made by chopping up the edible part of the cactus-bulbs and dumping them into a Waring Blender.

'Here, now,' said Fred Eichner, disturbed, when he reached her, 'my man will see to the buffet, you've only to —'

'The girl may be right, Fred,' said Marty. 'Anyway, better safe than sorry, eh?'

Dr Eichner seemed confounded and Martin Frost took his arm.

'You get comfortable, Fred, I'll see to the arrangements here,' and so saying he led the Doctor to a big deep cloth chair near where the girls were dancing and set him in it, and there the Doctor seemed to lapse at once into a sort of expectant coma, watching the graceful movements of the girls in dance and nodding his head and tilting it about, a pleasant smile on his face. The two girls moved throughout the large room, weaving a dreamy arabesque across the scene: and sometimes circling the Doctor's chair.

'Make it,' said Jean-baby to Frost when he went back to the sideboard, 'it's the proverbial end groove kick.'

'Hmm,' said Frost skeptically, frowning over the arrangements there, but he took one of the canapes, then grimaced painfully at the taste of it.

On the sideboard as well, bottle-dark in their yellow lacquered chilling-buckets, were several magna of champagne, one of which was open, and Jean handed him a brimming glass.

'Wash it down with juice, daddy, it's a gas.'

Frost swigged it down.

'Cut that argot,' he said to her quietly, 'or I'll break your head open.'

Jean arched her brows prettily and, with a toss of her head, left the sideboard carrying a tray of the prepared canapes which she proffered about among the guests.

Dr Eichner seemed doubly pleased at the sight of the canapes and at his idea of the way things were going generally.

'I don't entertain often,' he said to Jean as he accepted one, 'I will say an occasional affair such as this is pleasant.' He tried to move his arm in a gesture that would take in the scene, but only the hand flopped about momentarily.

'It's a real down gas,' said Jean, 'I'm hot to make that pepper kick.'

Behind them, Frost, having eaten several more of the wafers, had begun to examine things, walking slowly around the room, looking into drawers and under cushions.

'Who's that girl by the door?' he demanded of Jean and the Doctor when his investigations reached them. Dr Eichner didn't seem to hear him properly and kept beaming, nodding his head.

'Are you kidding?' asked Jean in a high voice, looking to where the girl swayed exotically. '*You* must be zonked out completely. That just happens to be a chick you set turning tricks for crissake!' She stared at him in amazement. 'What do you think you're doing, anyway, poking around the room like that?'

Frost looked impatient.

'This is a routine check,' he said, and moved on toward the study.

directly in front of him, at which time he would beam and sway his head.

There was an intentness in the way the girls danced, with no change of expression in their faces, and apparently without the least self-consciousness.

Frost came out of the study abruptly, carrying a shallow wooden box which he brought to the Doctor.

'Look at this,' he said, almost angrily, and knelt to place the box on the floor next to the chair. It was a wide felt-lined box and contained the Doctor's collection of miniature sports cars. Tiny, Swiss-made replicas, they were precision machined and finely detailed, all scaled to perfection, 1 : 1000, so that each was about the size of a small, oblong wrist-watch. Nestled together in the box, all silver-spoked and gleaming, richly enamelled and chromed, they resembled something from a jeweller's case.

Dr Eichner stared at them for a moment without reacting.

'Good,' he said then, '*very good*!'

He eased himself out of the chair and onto the floor.

'Very good,' he continued, 'very good.'

Rubbing his hands together, he began to take the cars out of the box and to range them about on the rug.

Frost stood up and watched him briefly.

'Good,' he said, and stalked away to where Jean was sitting in a corner, eyes closed, throwing palmfuls of pepper into her face, breathing it in hard, and occasionally gagging. She opened her eyes when Frost came up.

'Man nothing's happenin' with this jive, what you think that cat was puttin' down?'

'Cut the jargon,' said Frost, 'I'm sick of it.'

'You cut the jargon, daddy-o,' said Jean gaily, 'and I'll cut the horse,' and she threw a handful of pepper in the air and tried to catch it with her upturned face.

Frost gripped her shoulder. 'Head's up,' he said dramatically, looking darkly towards the door, 'it's the punk.' For at that moment, Treevly and his friend walked in. They were chatting amiably, like two earls strolling the Tuilleries.

Frost went forward to meet them.

'Good of you to come,' he said with a weird grimace, 'good of you to come.'

'Delighted,' said Treevly, 'delighted. A delightful place. Isn't it, Syl?'

'Yes, it's delightful,' said the other young man, who was somehow similar to Treevly, and while he did not quite have his style, he was well on the way.

Frost led them to the sideboard and indicated they should help themselves to the refreshments there.

'This *is* fun,' said Sylvester. 'Isn't it, Fee?'

'Fabulous,' said Treevly.

Frost himself ate several of the canapes quite hurriedly.

'I'll just see to things,' he said, opening a drawer of the buffet and peering into it.

Histoire du Soldat was playing now and, at the tango part, Treevly and the other young man began to dance. They danced eccentrically, marking the measure with a haughty and mincing step. Very soon they were actually prancing, like things possessed, faces frozen in serious mien.

It was so outlandish that it caught the attention of the three girls, who stopped and watched them in silence, nodding and applauding politely at the end, before playing the record over again.

Frost, however, went his own way, rummaging about the room, as did Jean-baby who was lying on her back now, one arm full length, dropping the pepper bit by bit, most of which was going in her hair. Frost then, after a moment's pause and a sudden look of complete wildness, plunged out of the room and into the depths of the house.

Under the effects of the mah-joong and peyote, Dr Eichner's concentration on the little cars was so whole that he had failed to notice Treevly's entrance and, even so, a few moments later had slipped forward and was now sprawled on his knees and face in a heap amidst the cars in a state of near coma.

It was then that Treevly, in executing some sort of fantastic dervish, stumbled over the Doctor and, half rising in a pique, recognized him. His reaction was very much like that of a cat.

'Eeechh!' he hissed through his teeth, leaping backwards and cringing against the sofa.

'J'accuse!' he cried, looking wild-eyed, pointing from his half crouch. *'Voyeur! Voyeur!'*

Dr Eichner, whose eyes were half open and shot with a comatose glaze, remained immobile, and seemed to hear only as one hears through a dream.

Treevly, in his turn, grew bolder and, coming forward from the couch, pointing again, turned to the girls and said: 'See here a man *obsessed*! It is a man . . . *obsessed*!'

His friend meanwhile had joined him and, standing over the Doctor, was making little incoherent sounds of derision and snapping his finger at the inert body in repetitive gestures of curt dismissal. Suddenly Treevly took his arm for support. 'I feel faint,' he said, putting his hand to his head. 'Oh, how I *detest intense* people!' he cried in real anguish. 'Oh, how I *loathe* them!' But as though the wave had passed, he drew himself up and spoke with menacing calm:

'Perhaps he hasn't had the last laugh, *after all*!'

And so saying, with a toss of his head, he was away again, he and his friend, lost in the dance, marking the measure with an imperious step.

upon Ralph kissed her anew.

Because of the extraordinary events of the evening, the couple had put off their plans for Monsieur Croque's, and half-past midnight found them still in the back seat of the convertible, having glanced at the screen scarcely a dozen times.

During the three presentations of *Wuthering Heights*, Babs had cried a lot, sometimes as in shame and need of reassurance, but mostly in soft bewilderment, and later in a kind of pitiful happiness. Now and again, however, she would sit up, quite suddenly, and turn her face away. 'You think I'm terrible,' she would say. This happened usually at the times when Ralph had moved over slightly to light a cigarette, or mix a drink.

'Don't be silly,' Ralph would say, kissing her affectionately, whereupon the girl would implore, 'Oh, Ralph, do you really . . . do you really *love* me?'

'Of course I do.'

'Do *what*?' she would want to be told.

'Do *love* you,' he would say.

And the girl would sigh and snuggle in his arms, as if she wanted nothing more than their being together like that always.

But the screen finally went dark, and while the national anthem resounded over the vast lot coming alive with crawling lights, Ralph suggested they go to a motel. And this seemed so scandalous to Babs that she burst into tears.

'Oh, you do think I'm terrible!' she sobbed. 'Oh, why did I do it? *Why*? You know I didn't want to, you know I *didn't*! You made me do it—you made me do it and now you *hate* me! Oh, I wish I were dead!' And she tried to bundle herself in the far corner of the seat, face hidden away, as Ralph stroked her hair and reassured her, bringing her face to his and carefully kissing the tears away.

On the porch of the boarding-house where Babs lived, she said they should not talk or kiss much there because of Mrs McBurney. But she made Ralph promise to call her next day at the Clinic, where she had Sunday duty, and she whispered finally, 'Ralph, you do believe me, don't you, that I had never . . . I mean, you do know that you're the only one who has ever . . .'

'Yes, I know,' said the boy, very pleased.

CHAPTER XXII

FRED EICHNER had no memory of how he had reached his bed the previous evening. He awoke, feeling very cross, with the taste of gall and waste in his mouth; it was almost noon.

'Put me on to Martin Frost,' he said, after snatch-

'Is . . . is this *Jean*?'

'Pardon?'

'Jean, *Jean-baby.*' The last words passed the Doctor's throat with the grotesque uncertainty there of a reversed fish-hook.

'This is an answering service. I understand that Mr Frost left the country. I understand, from one of the girls here, that—'

'Never mind,' snapped Eichner, recovering, 'this is F. L. Eichner, a client of Mr Frost. Please tell Mr Frost that I have no further need of his services. You may tell him to bill me, as of this date, and to consider his interest in the case closed. Is that clear?'

'Yes, sir.'

'Very well then. Thank you, and good-bye.'

'Good-bye.'

The Doctor replaced the receiver momentarily, then dialed the Clinic. It was Eleanor Thorne answered the phone.

'We've been trying to reach you, Doctor—at your home. There was no answer there.'

'I've been indisposed,' said Dr Eichner curtly. 'Why were you calling?'

'A police representative was here to see you.'

'What do you mean? An officer of the police?'

'Yes, Doctor, a policeman. An ordinary policeman, in a car. There were two of them. One remained in the car.'

'I see.'

'They wanted to see you.'

'*They?*'

'What?'

'All right, where are they now? They're no longer there I take it.'

'No, he said they would be back. I hope nothing is wrong, Doctor, I told him that you were *not* to be—'

'All right, now, I want you to go to my office. In the upper left drawer of the main desk you will find a list of the names and telephone numbers of certain agencies. When you have this list, call me here and give me those names and numbers. You may phone from my office. Is that clear?'

'Yes, Doctor.'

'Very well. Please do this as soon as possible. Let this case take priority over anything else you may have to do at the moment.'

'Yes, I will, Doctor.'

'Thank you, Nurse. Good-bye.'

'Good-bye, Doctor.'

Fred Eichner was out of bed in a bound. He put paper and pencil by the telephone, and had just entered the bathroom to begin his toilet when the phone rang. The Doctor was back to the bed and had the receiver up at once, pencil in readiness above the paper. 'Yes, go ahead.'

'I'd like to speak to Dr Eichner, please. This is Sergeant Fiske of the Los Angeles County Police.'

'I see,' said the Doctor, lowering his pencil.

'Yes, I remember you, Sergeant.'

'Yeah, well, they got those guys, Doc. You were right about that all right. The Chief said we ought to tell you as soon as we could get hold of you.'

'*What*? What's that you're saying?'

'It was a gang, trying to knock off somebody. "Good-Time" Gimp Spomini. He's got a car like yours. You see, they thought it was *you*.'

'You mean they thought *I* was *him*? *he*?'

'The Chief said to tell you it was a case of *mistaken identity*. They mistook you for him—because of the car, and because he was around there—he was supposed to be coming down that road then. His girl lives out there, you see.'

'I see! Good! Excellent! So the case is closed, is that it?'

'This case is closed, yes. They got him last night. He had a car like yours.'

'They got him? The rival gang got him? Killed him?'

'No, he's in the hospital. They say he'll be all right. But he identified them, you see, identified the rival gang. We got the whole bunch.'

'Well, I'm glad he wasn't seriously hurt!'

'No, he wasn't seriously hurt. He's a cripple . . . that's why they call him Gimp. "Good-Time" Gimp Spomini, he's called. Wanted. They're all wanted.'

'I see.'

'Well, this case is closed then, Doc; I mean, as far as you're concerned. The Chief said you ought to know about it. The Chief will probably call you about it himself.'

'Yes, of course. Well, I'm very glad you called, Sergeant. Meanwhile, convey my best wishes to youı Chief—for a job well done.'

'All right, Doctor, I will.'

'Is there anything else?'

'What? No, they just said you would want to know.'

'Yes, it's a great relief, of course. Thanks again.'

'That's okay. Well, good-bye.'

'Good-bye, Sergeant.'

The Doctor had no sooner put down the receiver than the phone rang again.

'F. L. Eichner here.'

'Doctor,' it was Eleanor Thorne calling, 'I've been trying to get you—'

'Nurse Thorne, you have that list: dispose of it. Into the wastebasket beside the desk with it! The case is closed, you see.'

CHAPTER XXIII

'WELL, Miss Smart,' Dr Eichner was speaking brightly into his inter-office phone, 'what's on the agenda for today?'

[illegible] and Mrs Richmond-White were two of several women who checked with him each Sunday to see if any new complexion-aids had been discovered during the past week.

Both their skins were perfect, a condition they attributed to proper diet and to the Doctor's prescribed methods of care—which had become, more or less, the focus of their lives.

As for Dr Eichner, he had, over the years, developed such an esoteric intimacy with their skins, that, through various tests and analyses he was able now to appreciate that, quite aside from their being perfect in the ordinary, unblemished sense, they were also *theoretically* perfect. This pleased his taste for the abstract, and, of course, his acute sensitiveness to points of dermatic structure.

Actually, these women were not very pretty. They were, for the most part, wealthy and well-educated; and their collective *gestalt* was a strict fascism, drawn solely on lines of skin-condition. Two vast hulks of society had been simply written off as 'starchy' and 'oily.' To describe what remained, a slang with quasi-humorous ramifications—that hallmark of organization—had evolved to include such expressions as 'ducking' (for 'duct-flow'), 'vel' (from 'velvet') for skin, 'salting the vel,' meaning a form of perspiration; and, in current usage among the more vulgar young were the obvious derisions 'grease-ball,' 'potato-face,' 'leather-tummy,' 'a real *imp*' (from 'impetigo'), 'a stupid *ex*' (from 'eczema'), 'a scroffy,' and so on.

In light conversation among themselves, for want of a more practical frame of reference they usually spoke of public figures, and in so otherwise an unbiased way as to frequently link persons like Madame Nehru and Jane Withers. More seriously, however, as in their visits with Dr Eichner, they spoke of 'stability,' and '*level*-problems.'

Dr Eichner would say: 'Yes, the endo is steady now, very steady.' Or, 'I want to try something, Miss Trumbel. Oh, we're on safe ground all right, but I've been toying with the idea of cutting down that ecto-lymph potential . . .'

About three-thirty Fred Eichner took tea alone in his office, followed by a quarter-hour's nap. He spent the next half-hour with his automotive correspondence, checking the run-down, point by point, on the latest performance sheets of a supercharged Pegaso and the Ferrari 375. After this comparative study, he perused the sheets more casually, making an occasional notation, however, on the margin of the sheet at hand. Finally, he paused and took up the inter-office phone: 'Miss Smart. For tomorrow, first opportunity: get the Alfa Romeo people, have them send their representative around with the 3-Litre Disco Volante — *after* confirming these figures: "Displacement — 145.24. One, forty-five point, two-four." That is the figure I want checked specifically. Motor Sheets lists a two-hundred b.h.p. at 6,000 r.p.m. for that displacement.

a close-fitting, beret style hat. A heavy layer of pan-stick covered her face and lips, so that there was no difference in colour between them, both being the same dull-glossed ochre; the periphery of the lips, however, was sharply etched by a thin crimson line.

'Mrs Gross?' said Dr Eichner, rising and extending his hand.

'How do you do, Doctor,' said Mrs Gross with a penetrating smile.

'Please sit down, Mrs Gross.' The Doctor regarded her studiously. He took her to be an actress almost at once. 'You were referred to me — '

'Yes, Doctor, by Mrs Winthrop-Garde.'

'Mrs Winthrop-Garde,' Dr Eichner repeated, striking an attitude of reflection.

'Of Washington, Doctor.'

Mrs Gross' eyes were not large, but brilliant blue they were set to advantage in a wide swirl of dark up-swept lashes beneath pearl-shadowed lids which were faintly iridescent. The lashes were almost theatrically false, while the brows above were drawn in a black arch of permanent surprise.

'But what can I be thinking of?' demanded Mrs Hugo Gross, bringing a black-gloved hand to her cheek in slight chagrin. 'I doubt that Mrs *Winthrop-Garde* was married at that time! Now what *was* her maiden name? We only met a short time ago, you see, and — '

'Oh, no matter,' said Fred Eichner genially, waiving the question with his hand. 'No matter at all! I was, I must confess, simply curious.' And he gave Mrs Gross a smile which caused her to writhe pleasantly, though with no serious loss of her rather gracious bearing. 'Well, now, Mrs Gross,' he continued, 'what, exactly, seems to be the trouble?'

'A skin-disorder of some sort, Doctor,' said Mrs Gross gravely, then went on, smiling in half apology, 'though I imagine you would have guessed as much! However, it's a form of *rash,* I suppose, occurring periodically — at no particular intervals — two weeks, three, sometimes as widely spaced as a month — on my stomach, and on my hips, the back of my hips —' Without being in the least coy, Mrs Gross displayed a certain half smiling modesty as she concluded, '— where I sit *down* is what I mean to say. It began about a year ago . . .'

'To your knowledge,' the Doctor took it up, 'were you ever subject to allergies? As a child, perhaps?'

'No, not to my knowledge, Doctor. Though there is something I think I might tell you. Up until a year ago, I was unbelievably *overweight.'* Mrs Gross began here a spritely narrative which, almost to the very end, she punctuated with acute facial expressions, little smiles, sometimes wistful, sometimes of delight, but never morose or dramatic, in spite of what she said. 'Not that I'm such a frail slip of a creature now! My weight now is 133. But a year ago, it was 255. Two hundred and fifty-five in the French class, during the individual recitations, we always stood by our desks in turn, and when we were finished, the Professor would say — he always spoke to us in French — *"c'est fait,"* or, if it had been quite good, *"c'est bien fait."* If it wasn't satisfactory, however, he would interrupt the recitation with *"c'est assez!"* or, if it was very bad, *"c'est bien assez!"* Well, on this particular day, I hadn't prepared my lesson — which wasn't like me at all, because I think I can say really quite objectively that I was a very conscientious student, and certainly above the average in French — but, on this occasion, there were circumstances which I needn't go into here . . . and I simply *wasn't* prepared. Well, he did interrupt — perhaps only to show how democratic he could be, since I *was,* after all, an exceptional student. *"C'est bien assez!"* he said. Before I could sit down, someone behind — I've never been certain *who* — said in a loud whisper, *"Mais oui, c'est bien assez — pour le monstre!"* I can tell you, Doctor, that phrase, just as it was spoken, with all its fault and childish intonation, has haunted me to this day! Well, I left school the next week. I became a sort of recluse, studying privately. Instead of taking books from the library, I bought them, always at different shops. I no longer saw any of my old friends, and changed residence often. I ate in a new restaurant every day — and *how* I ate! It was escape, recognition, defiance, indifference, security, *everything!* I remained — not happily though, I assure you — in this frame of mind for years — until, as I say, about one year ago when I read a *book,* a powerful book, *Know Thyself* by Dr Joseph Fineman. Oh, this will sound naïve to you, I'm sure, but — well, it gave me great hope and, as providence would have it, I received at about the same time an invitation to cocktails — from an all but forgotten friend, a schoolmate, perhaps of that very French class, *perhaps* even the very person who had spoken . . . In any event, I accepted the invitation. In the spirit of the book, I accepted. I *went* to the party. I arrived late. The door was open, the room was full — a gala crowd — and the hostess was not on hand, so I went in. As I crossed the room, I was obsessed by the phrase, *"Voila! C'est bien le monstre!"* I felt faint and sat down at once at the end of a large divan which was covered with fluffy scatter-pillows. A maid, passing with a tray of hors d'œuvres, stopped, and I took one and settled back on the divan. I sat there, silently, eating, looking straight ahead. Everyone around was engaged in conversation and seemed oblivious of my presence. I was thankful for that. Suddenly, however, I had the strange impression that I was *sitting on* something, almost as though — well, I casually, or should I say *cautiously,* looked behind me and assured myself that it was only one of the throw-pillows there, and I settled down again. I hadn't more than finished my hors d'œuvre though, when the feeling came over me again — I was so conscious of my weight, you see, and I was stricken with fear at the idea of …

… *warm* … up quickly and withdrew my hand! Then I reached for it again — I had to know, you see — and I managed to move the pillow slightly and have a peek. What was it? It was the body of a tiny dog, a toy Pomeranian, the smallest of creatures, and the dearest no doubt, of pets — suffocated, of course, by my great body. Well, to bring the story to a close, Doctor, I contrived to scoop the body into my handbag, unseen by anyone, and then walked hurriedly from the room, down the stairs, and into the street. At the first refuse-can, I emptied my handbag — of everything, all my cards, cosmetics, change, personal items, etcetera. And I walked home.

'After that, I couldn't eat. I became thin — as you see me now — in no time at all; almost, one might say, over night. And the day of the cocktail party was the day my rash began. *Does* the story amuse you, Doctor?'

Toward the end of the narration, Mrs Gross' smiles and gesticulations had become progressively exaggerated: she showed such an excess of teeth that they resembled snarls, and suggested pain. From moment to moment she arched her brows and grimaced terrifically, as in a pantomime for a wide, distant audience. The Doctor regarded her with growing scrutiny; there was something haunting, and frighteningly caricaturish about her at these times.

Mrs Gross had built to this, and as a climax, at the point of asking 'Does the story amuse you, Doctor?' she threw her head to one side and struck a pose, stone still, her stark face frozen in the distortion of a toothpaste advertisement, a face trapped at the very peak of a hysterical laugh; and the Doctor sat as one mesmerized with horror until the suspense was shattered by the woman suddenly reaching up and snatching at her hair, which gave way in her grasp, and the full horror smothered the Doctor, as in a valley filling from above with a mountain of snakes, that what was confronting him, laughing with sly insanity, was no less than Felix Treevly.

A little cry of terror broke from the Doctor before he shuddered and then lunged bodily at his tormentor, seizing at his throat with both hands in the desperate certainty that his mind would snap if he heard another sound from those lips. With an adroit sidestep behind the chair, however, Treevly escaped the thrust. 'The Doctor isn't telling all he knows' he whispered with fanatic intensity.

Dr Eichner grabbed the onyx paperweight and lashed out blindly. It seemed to just graze Treevly's brow, for he stumbled, and then fell forward, toward the desk. But in falling, Treevly must have struck his head against the lower part of the desk—for when the Doctor examined him, he was not merely unconscious, he was actually dead.

'I shouldn't wonder!' said Beth. 'Police all over, what's the place coming to?'

'Well, naturally we had to bring the Police into it. Unfortunate, I admit, but there it was.'

'Oh?'

'Oh yes, they worked with the private agencies on it.'

'Well! I'm certainly glad it's over and done with! Police crawling all over the place, snooping around! What must the patients think, that's what *I'm* wondering!'

'Really, Beth. I seriously doubt if anyone noticed. After all — '

'Oh, it was *noticed* rightly enough, no mistaking that! The radio in their car was so loud a body couldn't think. Hold-up here, accident there, drunks, fires, murders, and Lords knows what! Ha! And poor Miss Klein just out of surgery and running a temp. If my Miss Klein gets worse, I suppose we'll know who to thank for it!'

'There's been a complaint then?'

'She didn't say a word, El, bless the darling! The child's frightened to death as it is.'

'Well — '

'Oh, there were plenty who did notice, I can tell you! *And* small wonder, with their big car in my flower bed.

"You'll oblige these sick people by turning your radio down" is what I told the man. And during Mrs Burford's morning programme at that! "Operatic Highlights," El, you know how she loves it. I had to shut the *window,* warm as it was in that room, would you believe it? If we can't have fresh air at the Clinic, then where are we?'

'It isn't likely to happen again.'

'Well, thank the Lord for small blessings is what I would say to them!'

Earlier in the day, during a conference with Nurse Thorne and Mr Rogers, Beth Jackson had been more or less forced into accepting, on behalf of her department, responsibility for the lost invoice on a small shipment of crocks for gyno.

CHAPTER XXV

FOR A long moment, the Doctor stood by his desk, staring down at the lifeless body in pure amazement. Then, as his hand moved with a slow, crab-like involition across the desk toward the inter-office phone, the imagery in his mind's eye began to rise and sharpen in unfocused conflict, until suddenly, dark indecision locked his brain in a torment. He dropped into a chair and buried his face in his hands, a portrait of despair.

'Good Lord!' he said half aloud, 'out of the frying-pan and into the fire!'

at once to deliberation and planning.

He went to the window. It was the close of another beautiful afternoon : a gentle wind moved past the lengthening shadows of cypress and pine, while the white stone benches along the drive were still warmly opaque with the limping sun. There was no one in sight. Dr Eichner closed the window and turned away; and from this point forward he moved with quick, inflexible resolve, and assurance. After locking the door, he donned a pair of rubber gloves and a surgical apron. He quickly found Treevly's wig and put it back on the man's head. Next he removed the long black glove from Treevly's right hand, and then he picked him up bodily and carried him to the window, which he opened with Treevly's hand, pressing it firmly and carefully against the handle. He took the body to a side closet and set it inside, leaving the door of the closet open. This done, the Doctor returned to the desk and briefly examined the contents of the purse Treevly had carried; and then, from a glass case on the wall, he took a large scalpel, and after pressing the handle against Treevly's palm, he deposited it in the purse. Following this same procedure, along with the scalpel and the black glove, he put into the purse two hundred dollars which he removed from his own wallet, and four hundred dollars which he took from a drawer of the desk. From a side-board decanter, Dr Eichner measured off one half-pint of whisky, which he then transferred to the chamber of a Norwich stomach-pump. Back at the closet, he fed the tube of the pump into Treevly's mouth, and finally, reversing the pump's operational direction, the contents of the chamber into his stomach.

The Doctor next removed the right shoe Treevly was wearing, a heavy, low-cut English style walking shoe, and returned to the window with it. The bottom of the window was only two feet above the outside ground level which bordered the Clinic on this side with a dark-loamed flower bed. Opposite the window, the bed narrowed to about one yard's width where the soil, just freshly turned for planting, had a soft, oily look.

The Doctor, on his knees, holding the shoe far forward in his right hand, leaned out the window and was on the instant of imprinting it deeply into the soil near the opposite side of the bed when he hesitated and, then suddenly, withdrew his hand. This was the first wavering point in the Doctor's undertaking, and it set him aback. Something had caused him, intuitively, to withhold the impression of the footmark and, now, to revaluate the situation entirely.

Procuring a tape from his desk, he measured the width of the bed—forty-five inches. The average woman's normal step is twenty-five inches, the average man's, thirty. Certainly, it would not be infeasible for a print to appear there, on the far side of the bed, just at the edge — and yet, or so the Doctor could reason, considering the height of the sill, *and* the natural impulse to *step over* the immediately began, a heavy bluish grass of such close-cropped thickness, yet so buoyant withal, that, obviously it would not retain a print from a low-heeled shoe for more than a minute. So, leaving the bed untouched, Dr Eichner turned away from the window and replaced the shoe on Treevly's foot; and, finally, placing the purse inside the closet, with the body, he shut the door and locked it.

He then sat down at his desk and telephoned the Police, to report a theft of approximately six hundred dollars, cash money.

CHAPTER XXVI

BABS MINTNER moved through the day as through a dream, until, toward afternoon, she met Nurse Beth Jackson just outside gyno, and they were in each other's arms at once, Beth exclaiming surprise, but saying a minute later that she had intuitively sensed the child's awakening.

'Oh, Beth!' cried Babs, clasping hands to her bosom and beaming helplessly. 'Isn't it marvellous!'

'Yes, child,' Beth returned, near tears, 'yes, oh gracious, gracious,' and they both fell to weeping and stroking each other for comfort.

Nurse Thorne was off duty for a while and away, but she returned to the Clinic at about five, looking mannish and trim in a close-fitted tweed suit. The way she strode back and forth in Nurses Rest Room, she seemed in need of a short stiff crop to gesture with, strike smartly against her thigh, and clear away things confronting her.

'So!' She stopped near the window and turned to glare at Beth Jackson, who was sitting on the sofa, absently swishing a last mouthful of tepid coke through her teeth, something she had gotten in the habit of doing after meals, and now did, any time she had coke, on the simple reflex of a once removed association.

'So! It *has* actually happened! What a fool I was! What a blind fool! Oh!' Nurse Thorne was so angry she could have bitten herself.

'El, she's in a dream! It's a thing to behold! She's like a magic, bewitched thing! Oh, it took me back, you've no idea!' Beth tilted the empty glass, chuckling into it.

'And now I suppose she's *pregnant!*' said Eleanor Thorne as though the word were enough to make anyone ill.

Beth was wide-eyed. 'Oh, mind, I don't say they went as far as all that! Really, El, I do think — '

'Why not?' demanded Nurse Thorne, anxious to face the worst. *'Why not?* Bewitched! *Bewitched!* Oh, the hateful, hateful irony of it!' She pointed a prophetic, accusing finger at Beth Jackson. 'Mark my words,' she

…, staring out the window as he spoke into the phone, 'I can still see her. She has just reached the front gate and is turning — I can't see her now — it's difficult to be sure from here, because of the trees, but I *believe* she turned left. Left on Wilshire, yes. All right, I'll wait here for him. Yes, good-bye.'

The Doctor hung up, then got on the inter-office phone:

'Miss Smart. What was the name of the woman who was just here — the last patient. Well, let us say the one you *suppose* to be here now, yes. Mrs Hugo Gross. Had you ever seen her before? I see. Now, I know we have been lax about this in the past, Miss Smart, but from this day forward you will require, and verify, a reference from each new patient. Is that clear? Yes, your Mrs Hugo Gross just threatened my life with a Hanlon scalpel and left with six hundred dollars, out the window. That is correct. What? No, that has been done. Naturally I notified the authorities before calling you — that *would* be the normal procedure, would it not? I'm not primarily interested, you see, in the gossipy aspect of the incident. Now, a representative of the Police will be here shortly. There is no need for you to wait, but you might be of help in this way : if you would care to write down a description of what the woman was wearing. Knowing the nature of women, your cursory observations might prove to be more exacting on this count than my own. Yes, any details of her dress you can recall. Black gloves, etc . . . No, you needn't concern yourself with the face — I remember the face quite well. Yes, write it down and leave it on your desk. I will get it when the officer arrives. Yes, thank you. And you may go home. Yes, good night, Miss Smart.'

CHAPTER XXVII

A POLICE car arrived at the Clinic about five minutes later and two officers got out. It was Stockton and Fiske. Dr Eichner shook hands with them in solemn friendliness.

'Well, sure seems to be your big week, Doc,' Fiske was saying aloud with a wide grin.

Both men seemed a little strange in the new setting, Fiske gawking around, unabashedly testing the carpet with his foot, marvelling at its thickness, and Stockton looking rather tight and suspicious. 'This where you work?' he asked the Doctor narrowly, 'I mean, this where your practice is?'

Whenever the Doctor and Stockton spoke together, Fiske followed their remarks like a drugged person watching a fantastic tennis match. He seemed forever on the verge of shaking his head, slapping his thigh, and saying, with a soundless laugh, something softly in wonder.

job of play-acting on *her* part . . . *pretend-ing* to admire the instruments, but absently, you understand, as though they didn't really distract her from what she was saying. Then, as she finished her story, she was standing — just where you are now, Sergeant — by the instrument case, silent for the moment, her fingers idly, or so it seemed, toying a Hanlon scalpel — a surgical knife with a four-inch blade — which, I noticed finally, she was slowly *encircling with her hand.* And then, shaking her head slightly, and without looking at me, she said: "*No.* No, Doctor, there's only one way you can help me now — " and suddenly, and with surprising, really forceful agility, she turned, brandishing the scalpel, and walked quickly toward me, speaking between clenched teeth, " — by giving me the money you have in that desk!" Well! I can tell *you,* gentlemen, I was that much taken aback!' And the Doctor illustrated this by falling into a momentary attitude of limp helplessness in his chair. Then he straightened himself abruptly, and narrowing his eyes, as in serious reverie, continued, ' — not so much by the mere fact of the incident, but by the way it progressed, or rather, by its effect on *me.* What I mean to say is this: One would not imagine that a woman with a knife would be, well, particularly fearsome — certainly I wouldn't have — and yet, there was something so *convincingly menacing* about it, so . . . *athletic,* you might say, in the way she handled the knife, that I was, I admit, genuinely afraid for my life. Nevertheless, I did protest at first, hoping to reason with her, even denying that there *was* money in the desk. I started to get up from my chair — and in an *instant* she had the scalpel at my throat! In short, I gave her all the money in the office — about six hundred dollars — and she went out that window, like an animal.'

Fiske gave a low whistle and looked from the Doctor to Stockton and back again. Stockton, who had frowned up from his note-book only once or twice during the whole narrative, immediately strode to the window. 'This window, right?' he asked sharply, making a note in his book, though, actually, it was the only window in the room. He impulsively grasped the handle to push the window open a little more. Dr Eichner gave a slight start and was about to speak but checked himself.

'She went out this window,' announced Stockton, holding on to the handle now to support himself as he leaned out peering around. 'What kind of shoes would you say she was wearing at the time, Doctor?'

'I'm not absolutely certain, of course,' said Fred Eichner seriously, picking up a small slip of paper as he spoke, 'but I asked my receptionist for *her* description of the woman's dress, and here is her list — remarkable what women will notice — and she has: "brown calf, British laced flats, crepe sole" which I take to be the common variety of low-heel walking shoe, and correct, I daresay, since, in restrospect, I don't recall the . . . the *clickity-clack* sound of high-heels, customary with quite keen, or more precisely, that he was at a hopeless loss, but wished to convey the opposite impression. Dr Eichner handed him the paper. 'My own recollection of her dress is completely substantiated here and, as I say, greatly expanded. I think this paper might better serve as a "description" than anything I can say on the matter. I've studied it closely and can think of no further detail that — '

'Sergeant,' said Stockton, addressing his companion, 'call in this description to Headquarters.' He handed the paper smartly over to Fiske, who looked at him first in surprise, then said 'Right!' and started out of the office. 'Wait a minute,' said Stockton. 'I want this place checked for fingerprints. Tell them to send a man over for that.' He stared intently at the handle of the window he had been hanging onto, now musing aloud, ' — if she went out that window . . .' It was enough to make Fred Eichner sick to stomach.

'I get you, Stock,' said Fiske brightly. 'Right!' and he was out the door in a bound.

'Doctor,' Stockton took it up again, attempting to sound casual, 'you say nobody tried to stop this woman. I mean, you didn't yell or anything for somebody to stop her when she left.'

'The woman was dangerously armed, Sergeant,' said

the Doctor coldly. 'It was obviously work for no one but the Police Department.'

'Was this money insured?' demanded Stockton, not one to be easily duped.

The Doctor smiled tolerantly. 'I have the ordinary "loss against theft" insurance,' he said. 'I doubt if it applies in this case, however. I do happen to have the serial numbers on the four hundred dollars though — the money which was in the desk. Those numbers are included, you may have noticed, on the paper you've given Sergeant Fiske.'

Stockton had gone back to looking at the window-handle. 'Wait a minute,' he said suddenly, and ran out of the office, where his strident voice could still be heard: 'Fiske, hold up on that call!'

Dr Eichner sat back feeling strangely content. The story he had told about the theft was perhaps the only creative thing he had ever done in his life, and it had left him with a sense of wondrous exhaustion, feeling all clean and relaxed inside. It was so powerful in fact that, for a moment he wholly forgot about Felix Treevly in the closet. Then he came around again and took up his previous concern, looking first at his watch, then out the window.

Dusk had moved in like a dry fog and it lay bluish-grey on the stone benches and pebble drive. In half an hour it would be dark.

The Doctor was getting his hat and coat together when the officers returned.

'Well, I guess that will be all, Doctor,' said Stockton ruefully, his eyes avoiding the window. 'I'm not going to have anyone over here tonight for prints. I mean, of their car and gave them his hand in good-bye, with a word of caution. 'Take care,' he said, 'the woman is dangerous.'

'Oh, we'll get her for you, Doc,' Fiske assured him cheerfully, 'don't you worry.'

'Thank you, gentlemen, and good night,' said the Doctor, waving them on.

'Good night,' they replied in unison, Stockton sounding disgruntled as ever.

The Doctor stood motionless, his eyes on the departing car, and when it turned out of the gate, he started down the drive himself, walking rapidly.

At the boulevard, he boarded the first bus and rode a few blocks into the residential section neighbouring the Clinic. It was a mounting, circular drive, passing well-spaced, long lawned, two-story houses, with big family cars and convertibles parked in clusters all along the street. It was cocktail time.

In a seat near the rear of the bus, Dr Eichner slowly pulled on a pair of thin leather driving-gloves. A minute later, he got off the bus and began to walk. It was almost dark. He walked in the street, along the left-hand side of the parked cars, looking into them as he passed. And exhilaration that began at the touch of his feet on the pavement rose and grew within him until he had to fight to control the pounding of his heart and temples. He had walked past about fifteen cars, all in the first half of the block, when he stopped at one, and after a quick look toward the lighted windows of the house, he got in, switched on the keyed-ignition, and carefully drove away.

When the Doctor reached the Clinic, it was quite dark, though no more than a quarter-hour had elapsed since his departure. He parked the car shortly to one side the veranda and went inside.

Prim Miss Steven, the night receptionist, was at her desk in the foyer.

'Miss Steven,' said Dr Eichner firmly, 'would you please go round to West Wing Nurses Room and get my Miss Smart? Something rather urgent has come up, and —well, I'll keep an eye on the desk for you.'

'Of course, Doctor,' said Miss Steven and started out in a hurry.

The Doctor raced to his office, a few doors away. From his liquor cabinet he took a fresh bottle of whisky, of the brand he had introduced into Mr Treevly, poured off one pint of this and put it into one of his own office decanters; the half-filled bottle he put in his coat pocket. He then opened the closet, gathered up Mr Treevly and, keeping a sharp look-out all around, carried him through the empty foyer, onto the veranda, down the steps, and placed him on the back seat floor of the car. He returned to the front desk and penned this note for Miss Steven:

Miss Steven. Sorry to have troubled you. I was certain I had seen our Miss Smart going to Nurses Rest Rooms to run. Good night.

F. L. EICHNER

He went directly to the car, got in and drove out through the night. As the car swerved into Wilshire and headed for the mountains, the Doctor flicked open the glove-compartment, deposited the partially filled bottle of whiskey, and snapped it to.

Fred Eichner drove through the thickening dark without anxiety or apprehension. The automobile was a Kaiser-Darrin, waspish by comparison to the cars he was accustomed to, but it suited his heady mood. He reached the desolate mountain roads and began to climb, leaving the lights of the city far below. He drove steadily for half an hour, the only sound in the night the constant whir of the motor and the slow moan of rubber tyres gnawing the shoulders around the ever left-sweeping curves. The Doctor drove as by second nature, giving separate scrutiny to the characteristics of the road, especially inasmuch as they corresponded with warning markers that preceded them. Finally, at a sign reading: 'DANGER — Sharp Curve 200 feet ahead,' he slowed the car. Shortly beyond the marker, the headlights picked up the ominous white criss-cross of guardrail and red reflector lights. He stopped the car and got out to reconnoitre the site. It was a hairpin curve with a thousand foot drop about four feet beyond the rail.

The Doctor surveyed the area carefully, climbing the rail to examine the ground in front of the drop. It was a sheer haze of depth which, in the light of the rising moon, seemed milky soft, as though all the vast space and rock were under clear, warm water. In that moonlight, too, the Doctor's face seemed to have changed, indefinably, and when he returned to the car, he was visibly quivering with excitement. He got in, and without turning on the ignition, allowed the car to roll back about a hundred feet. He started up the engine, raced it terrifically several times, peering at the white rails dead ahead, then began the ascent, climbing fast, and faster, straight for the rails until at exactly the right instant he flattened the brake and put the car into a screaming twist as it smashed through the rail and came to a stop, veering sideways, two feet from the brink of the drop.

The Doctor sat still behind the wheel for a moment before getting out to look over his work. It was a first-rate job. He had crashed, almost sideways through the rail, leaving on the pavement behind a seventeen-foot black-burnt smear of anguish. All that was necessary now was to release the brake and over the vehicle would go. He cut the motor and put the car in gear, with the emergency brake on. After he had gotten out and hoisted Treevly into the front seat behind the wheel, he closed the doors and leaned inside; he turned on the switch, put the gear in third, and released the emergency.

The car started slowly forward and over it went, in a sort of lazy loop. At first it seemed buoyant, floating like sound at that distance.

Finally, after puttering about the ground near the ledge, arranging its disturbance to his purpose, he gave a brief inspection to the burnt tracks on the highway behind, and then started walking down the road. It took him almost three hours to get to a bus line, from whence he went directly home, had dinner, read for an hour, and slept then like a tired lover.

CHAPTER XXVIII

As for Babs Mintner, however, Ralph did not call her all during the day, and that night she cried herself to sleep.

Next day, by a remarkable effort of will, she stifled her impulse to be at the Dispensary at two o'clock sharp when he arrived. Instead, she waited one full hour before casually presenting herself there, as on business, for aspirin and pheno-barb.

And the boy seemed somewhat embarrassed when she did appear, but it was evident, too, that he was slightly disturbed at her not having come earlier.

'Hello, stranger,' he said, blasé, frowning a bit.

'Hello,' she said, feigning a friendly calm.

'Well' he said, *'you've* sure changed!'

'Why, how do you mean?' asked Babs, managing surprise.

'Well, if you don't know,' he said, looking hurt, but shrugging it off.

Babs fought to maintain a sane countenance, handing the boy her list of things.

'I wanted to phone you yesterday,' he went on, lightly now, almost wistfully, as he took the items off shelves around him.

'Well, we were pretty busy,' said Babs airily, regarding her nails.

'—but I had to go out of town,' Ralph continued. 'I called last night and they said you had gone to bed.'

'Oh?' said Babs, actually biting her tongue. 'They didn't tell me.'

'They didn't?' said Ralph, looking puzzled, as he came closer to the girl. 'Well, no, I guess I didn't tell them to.'

'You could have left a message,' said Babs, surrendering up to him with full wet eyes.

'Well,' said Ralph, not exactly ready to deaden his own pain, 'I thought I'd be seeing you *sooner than this.'*

'Did you?' she demanded, snatched up her things from the counter and marched away.

But alone, in Nurses Rest Room, she could only think of *him*; and it was frightening for her as though with every image the new-born thing inside her grew gradually out like some kind of weird plant towards a huge and unshe sauntered past Ralph, her eyes [illegible]antly perusing the list in her hand.

'Babs,' he called in tender despair.

'Oh!' She gave a slight start, looking up, even as rather surprised to find him there.

'Please, Babs,' he begged, motioning her to come over. 'Why are you being like this?' He was clearly disturbed, but more sure of himself now that she was actually there.

'Oh, we've been so busy, you've no idea!' said she, touching her hair as she approached, frowning down at her list.

'Oh? What's up?' the boy asked, attempting to go along with it, arching his brows.

'Oh, it's Fred again — Dr Eichner,' lied Babs easily.

'Yeah? What's the matter with him?' asked Ralph, trying to make the fanatic jealousy in his face pass for amused interest.

'Well,' Babs began, glancing around the corridor, 'there's been some trouble. I — I can't talk about it now.' And she gave him a quick, dark look to sharpen the mystery of it.

Ralph seemed on the verge of a strong reply, but suddenly the corridor sounded with a patter as the ward-boy, Albert, came up on the run, making small animal noises the while. Babs put out her hand caressingly, just as one might to intercept the flight of a dear little puppy dog, completely ignoring Ralph now in making much of the dwarfed near-mute who, with childish ferocity, began at once to pummel her stomach and tug at the skirt of her habit, sometimes exposing the sweet secret ruffles beneath.

'Don't let him do that!' begged Ralph furiously, leaning across his counter toward them.

'Shh,' Babs said, 'he's trying to tell me something.'

Albert looked up at Ralph in brief contempt, and then buried his face in the girl's skirt.

'Oh, the darling, the darling,' she murmured, closed-eyed, stroking his great head.

Ralph watched, in speechless wrath, as Albert tugged and beckoned Babs away, as to a tryst, and she feigning helplessness, allowed him to do so.

'It may be something about Fred,' she explained to Ralph.

'I'll be by for you at eight-thirty,' said Ralph with a firmness that shook his voice, 'I've got two tickets for a concert at the school.' And he withdrew them from his shirt pocket as proof of it.

'All right, dear, I'll see,' Babs called back lightly, as if too deeply engaged now to give it much thought.

'Eight-thirty,' Ralph commanded, glaring a really hateful vengeance at the back of the giant head of the dwarf, resting as it did against the hip of his own beloved.

more exactly, that it had been definitely established through the remnants of certain bills of currency found at the scene of an automobile wreck that the stolen money had been destroyed in the amount reported, and that a claim-slip for that sum was being processed and sent forward by the authorities. And, in due order, the Doctor would get full reimbursement from the Treasury Department.

No further comment was offered on the case at the time, the truth being that the authorities were desperately trying to prove a theory that the wholly unidentifiable body found in the wreck was that of the notoriously long-sought 'Black Dahlia.'

And now, in the middle of the afternoon, after the Doctor had been further informed that, as a formality, he would be asked to identify the scalpel, a plain clothes detective came round to the Clinic with it.

This detective looked more like a manufacturer's public-relations man than anyone's notion of a real detective. With a certain naïveté, he spoke in patient, explicative tones, avoiding those details which he thought the Doctor might find unsavoury. He was evidently rather embarrassed at having to say that the *woman* was not actually a woman, but a man so disguised.

'He was a maniac,' said the detective apologetically.

'You're lucky, I guess, that he wasn't more violent at the time. But you did exactly the right thing, simply giving him the money. You see, the amount was probably more than he expected and diverted his real intention — to put him in a good frame of *mind*, so to speak.'

'He had a record of violence, did he?' asked Fred Eichner in interest.

'Well, not *exactly*. We talked to his psychiatrist —'

'I see. He was under treatment?'

'Well, he *had* gone to this psychiatrist . . . and *he* wasn't surprised; I mean, he said he had known for a long time that the man was unstable which is certainly an understatement even so. Though naturally, the psychiatrist might tend to minimize it — afraid he would incriminate himself for not having advised the man to be locked up in the first place. But, of course, we had no such things in mind. We were only interested in the facts of the particular case. Actually, the department puts very little stock in what a psychiatrist may say anyhow — especially after the fact, so to speak. We have our own psychiatrists, of course. For the department, however, it is simply a case of theft-and-recovery.'

'You say she — rather *he* stole a car after he left here?'

'Yes. He came here — on some mad obsession — then was diverted from this obsession when he saw the scalpel. He wished to use it, but could not find the emotional strength or the reason — if I may use the word for a madman — to do so. He hoped you would provoke his anger by refusing him money, and thereby give him an excuse to do so. When you did not, but gave him six hundred dollars instead, his plan changed abruptly. He left, stole

‘Drinking, was he?’

‘Yes, a piece of a whisky bottle was found. He *might* not have been drinking before he came here. Not that you could have told, anyway. Whisky doesn’t affect a maniac the same as an ordinary person, though, of course, in some cases it may be worse.’

‘I *see.*’

‘Well, I guess that’s all there is to it. You should be hearing from the Treasury Department by the end of the week. I’ll leave the scalpel here, it belongs to you. It seems to be all right—about the only thing that survived the wreck, I’d say. Pardon me for saying so, but you ought to keep those things out of sight. I mean, you don’t want to give anyone more ideas.’ He stared at the scalpel for a long moment.

‘Yes,’ said the Doctor, ‘you’re probably right there. Well, good-bye and thanks again.’

‘You’re welcome. Good-bye.’

Dr Eichner took four o’clock tea and a sandwich. He had just settled, half-reclining on the leather sofa, with a brandied black coffee, for a comfortable half-hour of perusing his medical journals when the inter-office phone rang. It was Miss Smart to say that the published information on the Alfa Romeo trial sheets was in error, and that a supplemental erratum slip was being issued by the company, with apology.

'Very good,' said Fred Eichner, 'very good.'

'They say,' Miss Smart continued, 'that they would like to send a man around with the new model, anyway. They're sure you would be pleased with it. They're on the line now, Doctor.'

'No, that won't be necessary. I know this model quite well, you see. I was merely interested in getting at the truth of the published specifications. Ask their representative for the correct figure, please.'

'Yes, Doctor, one moment.'

While waiting, Dr Eichner fetched out his automotive papers and quickly located the sheet in question.

'Yes, Doctor, the correct displacement is: one, sixty-five, point, two-four. The other specifications are unchanged.'

'One, sixty-five, point, two-four. I'll just note that. Yes. Well, even so, that is a considerable gain over their last model, you see. But that hardly, ha! — hardly attains it to the — to the *Bugatti* class! You may tell him *that*. No. No, I won't require a demonstration of this model. You may say, however, that through the published reports, I am appreciatively aware of their progress and will, of course, be in touch with them as soon as — well, as soon as they *come-up-with-something*, so to speak.'

'Very well, Doctor. I'll tell them.'

'All right, Miss Smart. Now then, what time is it?'

'Four forty-five, Doctor.'

'My next appointment?'

'Why, there's nothing else today, Doctor.'

'Good. You needn't disturb me again, Miss Smart.'

discourage any undue forwardness on her p

'Take coffee, Miss Thorne,' he said, having already poured off two brandies neat. 'You have heard of the fantastic events of yesterday, no doubt?' he continued, drawing chairs together for them.

'Yes, what an extraordinary thing!' said she, trying to feel at home. 'Was it actually the man who came here before — intoxicated?'

'Evidently,' said the doctor, '*evi-dent-ly.*'

'He must have been mad. Really *mad*. It's — frightening.'

'My dear,' said the Doctor, smiling, putting a hand on her own, as both repressed a shudder of distaste, 'perhaps there's more of madness in the world than one can ever know, and *power* is not infrequently her bedfellow.' They raised their cups, each now using two hands for it, and the Doctor continued in a lively voice: 'However, I suppose the fortunate thing is that psychotic manifestations generally cause no alarm. Or is it *unfortunate*?'

'Well,' said Nurse Thorne, turning in her chair, 'I simply wanted to express my own—and I'm sure I speak for the rest of the staff — my own feelings of relief and gratitude that you weren't harmed.'

Dr Eichner nodded appreciatively, and Nurse Thorne went on: 'The money was recovered as well, I understand.'

'Yes. Yes, the money was recovered as well.'

There was a moment of silence while they both sipped of coffee or brandy before Nurse Thorne spoke again. 'Doctor,' she began earnestly but rapid enough to suggest that she had rehearsed. 'I hope I may speak to you in confidence. As you know, I have always admired your work here at the Clinic, and since being Head Nurse, I have come to have a great respect for you personally. I feel somehow closer to you than to most of the staff, and—well, I thought perhaps you would like to know that you will be asked to stay over for a board meeting this afternoon and—and to replace Dr Charles, as Chief Surgeon, when he retires next month.'

The Doctor took a delicate sip of brandy. 'Well! I must say that from time to time I had envisioned as much—on the basis of rumour, of course—but have managed to restrain my hopes so as not to be disappointed. May I ask where you heard this, Nurse Thorne?'

'It is no longer a rumour, Doctor. Sally Weston in the front office—she does Mr Roberts' typing—told me, in confidence of course. The meeting is to be at 5.20, in a very little while now. There was bound to be a leak.'

'Yes. Yes. Perhaps. Pertinent hearsay of the last minute should often be treated as conclusive. That is so. Well, Nurse Thorne, we will be working together, then.' The Doctor raised his glass, assuring her of it. 'My compliments,' he said.

Eleanor Thorne beamed, joining the toast.

'There may be some reorganizational matters wanting our attention later,' said the Doctor with great under-

'Thank *you*, my dear. Forewarned is quite [illegible] they say, *forearmed.*'

At five o'clock Dr Eichner had an emergency call from one of his regular patients, which he shortly concluded with the gentle admonition : 'I see what we're up against, Mrs Cranell. Your starch estimate did not take into account *soya,* and — well, I *think* we'd-better-*watch-it* for a week or so.'

Miss Smart then called to say that the Doctor was requested to stay over for a board meeting at 5.20. Miss Smart rather shyly repeated the hearsay, which, by now, was going the rounds with open, official sanction.

Dr Eichner settled down again, this time in a great leather chair, with his automotive trial sheets. He had just decided to replace his Delahaye with a new Gordini, and the decision made him tingle. Then, in a moment of reflection, he rose and went to the window. Half in a world of fantasy, his mind's eye roved the desolate winding heights of Andorra, and the endless moon-lit roads of Spain, where one could drive for a hundred miles without meeting a single car.

'You have bad luck,' said Garcia from below.

The Doctor gave a start. He had not noticed this Mexican gardener, puttering there in the bed below.

Garcia tipped his hat, smiling a little.

'Well, how are you, Garcia?' asked the Doctor.

The gardener nodded his head, smiling. 'You have bad luck,' he repeated, 'losing the money.'

'Yes, wasn't it,' said the Doctor with grand good nature. 'However, it's been found. They *found* it, the Police.' He spoke rather loud, as though the gardener were deaf.

'Yes,' said Garcia, 'the Police.' He nodded to show comprehension, making his smile a funny little twisted thing.

'*I need* money,' he said.

'How's that?' said Fred Eichner.

'I have twenty-three dollars a week.' He held up his fingers. 'Two-three,' he said. 'I need twenty-six. My wife have baby.'

Dr Eichner nodded in sympathy, but didn't speak.

'Twenty-six,' the gardener repeated, raising his fingers. 'Two-six.'

'Yes. Well, you should certainly speak to Mr Roberts' office about it. I'm sure they would see—' The Doctor stopped short, looking intently now at Garcia, as the latter stood shaking his head, still smiling, of course, rather artificially it would seem.

'You Doctor,' he said, pointing a finger at Fred Eichner, 'you will speak?'

'Well,' said the Doctor, 'it's hardly my place to ask the—'

'You new boss in Clinic, yes?'

'Perhaps,' said the Doctor, letting his annoyance show. 'But it would hardly be my place—'

'My wife no have baby,' said Garcia flatly. 'Already

ner had poised the low-heeled shoe of

'Footprint?' said the Doctor softly. '*What* footprint?'

'Footprint-of-thief,' said Garcia with slow emphasis. 'Footprint-of-woman-steal-money.'

And the eyes of the two men locked in steady fascination.

'There was a footprint there?' said the Doctor, incredulous at what was taking place. 'Yesterday?'

'Yes.' The gardener's smile looked strange and mechanical. 'I cover. Old seeds no good, eh? New seeds. Money.' He made a gesture then of holding his open palm out to the Doctor. 'You speak to Robert office please?'

'*When* did you find the footprint?' Dr Eichner demanded in a hollow voice.

'When thief run, I see. Thief jump into flower and run, yes?'

'You *saw*?'

'Yes. *I* see thief run.'

'You *saw*,' the Doctor repeated dully.

The gardener's laugh was like that of a wooden device. 'I see thief run,' he cried with grotesque gaity. 'I find footprint! Cover! Police, yes? *Police*! Police look for footprint. I cover. Yes? Footprint is cover!'

The Doctor's eyes left Garcia's and for a long moment seemed to scan the dim horizon of the closing day. He cleared his throat. 'You say—you say twenty-three to twenty-six?'

'Yes,' said Garcia, 'twenty-six. Two-six.'

'I think it can be arranged,' said the Doctor evenly. 'Yes, I think it can be arranged.'

The gardener turned to go, touching his cap. 'Little, yes? Yes. Two-six.' He gave the Doctor a very cool smile. 'Seeds not much cost! Seeds not much cost this year.' And he walked away slowly, into the dying light, rubbing the trowel against his leg.

CHAPTER XXX

THE CONCERT at the school was at ten o'clock, and when Ralph telephoned Babs about two hours before he was to pick her up, she had asked, lightly enough, if they were 'going formal,' whereupon Ralph had laughed, saying 'no, *au contraire*!' Even so, when Ralph went by for her, she appeared at the door wearing a new hat, high heels, and her smartest black, whereas Ralph was dressed simply, in the student manner of sports-jackets and open-collar shirts.

When she was settled in the car, Ralph gave her a kiss, but Babs pulled away, saying: 'Careful, don't muss!' And they were off.

Above the windshield, on the girl's side of the car, was a sun-shade, the back of which held a mirror, and snapping on the overhead light, Babs turned the mirror down to check her appearance. As the car got under way, she even adoration.

It was something quite beyond vanity. It was, in fact, as though she were very earnestly trying to take the boy and herself seriously, and that by continually referring back to her image in the glass, she could generously give whatever they might say the reality and the dramatic validity it could not otherwise have.

By the time they reached the school, Babs' animation had progressed to an extraordinary point, so that upon entering the auditorium, she received the immediate attention of everyone near, but most especially of the girls. And about half the audience *was* constituted of young girls, living on campus, here now in groups of two or more, attired in varying combinations of sweaters, jeans, men's shirts, sandals, skirts, short white socks, and saddle-shoes. Many had books with them, to indicate they had just come from the library, and some continued to read, while here and there were kerchiefed heads to show that these girls had freshly washed their hair or otherwise prepared it for bed.

There was a small army of single men in the audience who, for the most part, wore T-shirts, read from folded newspapers, and had a pencil behind one ear. Others were there, of course, in boy-girl couples, holding hands and talking gravely.

It was the girls, however, who were the motif of this scene. They turned and twisted in their seats, laughing to left, right, and behind, whispering, signalling with mystery and import. The girls were grouped, of course, and these groups seemed to vie with one another as to which could laugh the more often, with the most bitterness, and with the most emphatic finality. They leaned across each other, whispering things to which the others gave bent attention, then all would laugh with such a burst of savage and somehow sexual derision as to give the impression that what had just been said could only have been the most sensational obscenity conceivable to them, a peripheral *bon mot* relating to some fantastically heinous perversion of the Dean.

'Do you like Bach?' asked Ralph, looking over the programme.

'Love him!' said Babs, perhaps a bit too loud.

Several titters were heard and a girl, sitting slouched next to Babs, a lean, dry-lipped, sloe-eyed blonde whose shorn locks bunched their fullest an inch above her eyebrows, looked up from a book by Jean Genet, her mouth set in a pained distant smile.

'Why didn't you tell me it was going to be casual?' Babs asked in a disturbed whisper.

'But I did,' protested Ralph.

'But I mean like *this*!'

'Well—'

Then the music began. Babs sat stiffly upright through the piece looking straight ahead. When it ended, someone behind her said 'Oh, love him!' in a harsh stage whisper. And Babs joined in the light applause, trying to smile, high on her head, and her sightless eyes still wide in the effort to ignore the nudging and giggling among the girls.

They didn't speak then until they were in the car again.

'Sorry you didn't like it,' said Ralph casually, showing a foolish annoyance, and Babs burst into tears, hiding her face in her hands and pulling away from the boy at once when he tried to console her.

'You're ashamed of me,' she sobbed.

'What?' said Ralph.

'You *are*,' she insisted, pathetically, '— because — because I'm not in — *intelligent*.' She said this uncertainly, as though it might have been the first time she had ever had occasion to use the word. '. . . because I never *went* to college — you think I'm — *I'm nobody* — but I *wanted* to go — I wanted so much, Ralph —' and she raised her tear-traced face to him to plead the truth of it, '— and to be — to be —' but her voice trailed off in pitiful helplessness.

'Don't be silly,' said Ralph, slightly unnerved, if only by the singular close-up of a girl in a smart hat crying in real anguish.

'Don't be silly,' he repeated softly, kissing her eyes and cheeks, whereupon Babs herself may have sensed the incongruity for, a moment later, she pushed away from him to remove the hat, shaking her head, bringing a hand to her hair in little gestures of arrangement, which seemed to calm her wondrously.

Ralph started the car, and they drove down Wilshire Boulevard. Babs sat quietly, her face toward the window on her side, where the dead-dark trees fled past.

Neither spoke for a long while, and then they were parked on a thick-wooded hill overlooking the sea.

With the top down, it was a beautiful spring night; a full-rounded moon, all golden pink, lay low against the endless blue water like a great dripping orange.

'Does the moon look flat to you, or round?' asked Ralph.

'I don't know,' said the girl sadly, looking at the moon.

He took her hand, and there were only the sounds of the tide-swept shore below, and the wind.

'Do you . . . do you love me?' he asked with a soft finality, as though these might somehow be his very last words.

All around them steeped the lazy depth of grass that strove gently toward shades of cobalt near the earth, unthreatened now and forever by a moon made soft through the light night-driven clouds and, seemingly too, by a wind that stirred the jacaranda above with a motion and sound no less languid than the caressing breath of the girl.

'Why, how do you mean?' she asked, seemingly really ingenuous.

It was almost midnight and, everywhere now, small night-birds were beginning to flutter and, finally, to sing.

'The way . . . I love you,' said the boy.

And the birds sang, softly, and in a way, too, that did

CHAPTER XXXI

DR EICHNER lay in his own big bed, in the total darkness of his room, fully awake. On the night-table and scattered over the counterpane were about seventeen magazines.

The Doctor had retired at nine and had read for a while before turning out his lamp. He had fallen asleep straight away and had slept soundly for several hours, only to wake up suddenly, long before scheduled.

For five minutes he lay quite still, peering up into the darkness. Then he threw back one half of the top part of his counterpane, down from his shoulder to a diagonal across his chest, raised himself to one elbow, leaned toward the night-table, snapped on the lamp first, and then the dictaphone. He picked up the mouthpiece, made a final adjustment to a dial on the set, switched off the lamp, and lying flat on his back, in absolute darkness, began to speak:

'A letter, Miss Smart, to:

Editor

Tiny Car.

17 rue Danton

Berne, Switzerland

Dear Sir:

In your issue of 17 January you feature the article, by Jock Phillips, "Should Miniature Cars Run?"

First, let me say that I have *read* this article, that is to say, I have read . . . strike out the last seven words, Miss Smart. Period. Without referring directly to this article, however, let us consider the veritable host . . . the veritable *host* . . . underscore "host," Miss Smart . . . veritable *host* . . . do not repeat it, however . . . the veritable *host* of implications posed here which might best be treated categorically, that is to say, in the strict sense of . . . *category*. Underscore. Period. Now, by way of preface, let us take . . . let us take . . . but do not repeat it . . . let us *take* . . .'